NOVA
AND THE
GHOST

A HAUNTED HALLWAYS MYSTERY

LISA COURTAWAY

ISBN: 978-1-7374222-4-2(ebook)

ISBN: 978-1-7374222-5-9 (print)

Editing and Formatting by Two Birds Author Services

www.twobirdsauthorservices.com

Cover Design by Miblart

www.miblart.com

Author's Note

Our youngest child and only daughter was diagnosed with celiac disease after an acute illness put her in the hospital for more than a week; this was before she was eighteen months old. We had never even heard of celiac disease and had no clue what gluten was. To say we were blindsided would be an understatement, as would saying we were grateful. There were far worse diagnoses being brought up, so celiac disease seemed manageable and was far less dire than other potential illnesses.

Since her diagnosis, we have learned so much and our drive to keep our daughter healthy is unwavering. In this book, I wanted to share with readers the seriousness of being diagnosed with a severe allergy or auto-immune disease, while balancing those realities with the relative normalcy of one's existence with such a health issue. Like many things, our family regards our daughter's disease with large doses of comedy. Thankfully, she is a good sport! The characters in this story also use humor. This is not meant to offend anyone; it is just our way.

In Chapter 12, there is mention of a 504 Plan. Section

504 upholds the right to full access and participation in regard to education and school-related activities. It requires schools to provide appropriate services to meet the needs of qualifying students. For children with celiac disease, this can cover a wide range of provisions ranging from food items offered through school meal plans to things like gluten-free art supplies, unfettered use of school restrooms, sick day leeway and much more. We have been fortunate in the sixteen-plus years since our daughter's diagnosis to not have to utilize a 504 Plan. The elementary school she attended went above and beyond to keep our daughter safe and healthy. We were comfortable in the knowledge that had we felt the need to implement a 504 Plan, it was available.

As this is a ghost story, there is a death. It is not a gory scene, but it is moving and some could find it disturbing. Please use this information as you would like. As an author, my goal is to evoke emotion and I believe the scene in question accomplishes this mission. Having said this, if you know that such a scene may be too much for you, please select another story. Whatever you do, keep reading! Enjoy!

Prologue

Alone. The girl dwelled alone in the room. For many years, she'd existed in this solitary place—forsaken, forgotten. She wrote things on the wall of the dusty attic room. Reminders. Never would she have dared to write on the walls in her old life. Her real life. But her memory failed as her spirit remained trapped inside the cluttered attic of the school, an area long deserted and forgotten, closed off from the lively world beyond its door.

The first thing that threatened to fade from her memory was her name, so she scratched it into the wall. Under her name, she etched her birthday when she realized she'd begun struggling to recall the date. One thing she did not forget was the day she died. But she scrawled that date on the wall all the same, not knowing if anyone would ever see her crudely scratched letters and numbers —but hoping someone would.

There was another name she whittled into the shiplap too, a name she knew she would never forget. But the name needed to be there in case another set of eyes fell upon her intently etched history.

She wasn't sure how long she'd remained in the old school, the place where she took her last, gasping breath. How she wished she could simply stay trapped in her home. Certainly, the eternal loneliness would be more bearable in a place she cherished. Not like this dreaded space.

The worst of it all was she'd been forced to say goodbye to a life she loved.

At times, she grew bored with her solitary existence and drifted off into what she told herself was a hibernation of sorts, for they were long periods spent in a kind of dreamy sleep. During these spells when her mind wandered, she would find herself at the home she longed for, watching her family move on, watching her parents grow old. She wished she could stay there, but the sadness in her mother's eyes was agonizing and left her fearing that her mother sensed her presence. Never wanting to make things more painful for her beloved parents, she felt forced to return to the dark and dusty confines of the school's abandoned attic.

Once when her mind visited her home, she discovered something had changed. Her beloved dog, Orla, was gone. On prior dreamy homecomings, she knew Orla saw her and smelled her essence. The dog would stand in front of her, tail between its legs, pleading whimpers escaping between barred teeth. She would bend to pet her dog, but Orla ran from her. No more.

On a future visit, she spied her mother sitting in the soft grass in their backyard, the spot shaded by a cluster of fruit trees her father planted when she was very young. Her mother's attention fixated on a small imprint in the grass as she tugged at barely sprouted weeds and brushed her hand over the hallow, clearing it of fallen leaves and dirt. The girl never exited the house to explore the backyard, to venture to the garden she once tended to with her sweet mutt Orla by her side. Something told her she didn't want to see what lay out there that had become so important to her mother.

On yet another wander through her home, she stopped on the stairway to look at the family photos. There was a bare spot on the wall, a perfect rectangle where the wallpaper looked brighter because for years her school photo frame protected it from sunlight and dust. Twelve small, rounded cutouts ringed a large oval where her senior picture would have gone had she been given the chance to make it past the eighth grade. It was a loving record of how much she changed each year as she grew older. The bad haircuts, toothless smiles, changing styles—a progression of life, something her mother cherished. The frame was gone now. Four spaces would forever remain void of her smiling face.

At that moment, a tidal wave of grief engulfed her. She mourned for her parents more than for herself. How had they managed to move on? Perhaps they hadn't; they weren't living, only existing.

The last time she visited home, her mother and father were gone, as was the well-recognized furniture—the bed she'd been scolded for jumping on when she was little, the couch where she cuddled with her mom to read books on rainy Sunday mornings. The only familiar thing that remained was the porch swing her father hung. Someone had covered its dulled, chipped paint with a new glossy coat of bright red. Unfamiliar faces beamed back at her from frames on the walls. It confused and saddened her, so she stopped her mind from roaming those halls during her lengthy naps.

With her parents now gone, she longed to leave too. She knew there was someplace else she should move on to, a place where her mother and father might be waiting for her. Yet the need to have her story told kept her bound to the school, waiting for the right person to find her and set her free. She believed it was only a matter of time, and time was all she had. One day that person would arrive, and she saved her energy so when the moment came, she could, with all her might, reveal what happened all those years ago. She would fight for her cause no matter what the consequences.

A key hung on a rusted hook just inside the attic door. She believed the key, a creepy skeleton key dulled with age and covered with nicks and scratches, fit the attic door. She had no use for it. She moved easily through the school whenever she chose. Most times, though, she lingered in the attic. It stayed quiet there. She did venture out during school performances, listening to the choir or watching a play or talent show on the old stage two floors below her attic room. While listening to the children sing, she would close her eyes and imagine she stood on the stage, singing loudly with her peers as she had done so long ago.

The passage of time was evident in the children who attended the school and the cars that dropped them off each morning and rushed back at the end of the day. Even the school buses changed, becoming more streamlined despite being shaded in the same bright yellow as the one she rode on so long ago. The kids wore different styles of clothing, and most of the cars became smaller and sleeker. Hairstyles changed, and as of late, more and more children walked absentmindedly from their cars to the school entrance, engrossed in small electronic boxes they held in their hands. At times they would hold the small items out at arm's length and don fake smiles or pout their lips, holding up peace signs and freezing their poses for a moment. They did these things alone and in groups. No one talked to each other much. Whatever drew their attention to the item in their palms must have been far more interesting than conversations with their friends. The children were hypnotized by the small screens. Some wore headphones like the ones her father used to connect to his turntable. But the kids didn't have turntables, so she wondered what the headphones were for.

Today she lay asleep, having become immune long ago to the jarring school bell, the angry car horn blasts, and the shouts of children. As she lay there, drifting off into nothingness, a voice whispered two words in her ear.

"She's here!"

She moved to the dormer and gazed out the window. Amid the frenzied morning routine, her eyes were drawn to one girl—a new student who stood alone, appearing almost lost. Not knowing how but knowing for certain this was the one who would help her, she was powerless to avert her eyes.

Chapter 1

Nova Eckley stood outside the school on a blustery winter day, her stomach in knots. Drab, ashen leaves gathered in a whirl around her feet, drawn to her motionless figure by an icy blast of wind. Her mother dropped her off moments before with a peck on the cheek.

"Enjoy your first day! You're going to do great, hon!" her mom chirped.

That sunny attitude did nothing to encourage Nova, but she knew her mom was struggling with her own first-day jitters. Still, her mom would never understand how nervous she was about starting a new middle school on the first day back after winter break. All the kids would already have their friendships and cliques. There had been no chance to meet anyone new since she and her mother moved into their cramped apartment a few days after Christmas; a Christmas she'd rather forget—the first spent without her father. The worst of it all was she'd been forced to say goodbye to a life she loved.

As Nova stood alone under the gray sky, staring at the menacing building, she didn't notice the girl watching her from a small dormer window on the top floor of the old brick structure.

She didn't hear the rowdy group of kids behind her until a short boy bumped into her after his friend gave him a rough nudge. The contact drew Nova out of her thoughts, spurring her into action. She inhaled deeply, righted her backpack on her shoulders, and moved toward the stone stairs leading to the heavy wooden doors of the school. The boy threw an apology over his shoulder as he caught up to his friend and shoved him in playful retaliation.

Nova was pushed along through the crowded hall as she searched for her first-period classroom. A rush of rosy-cheeked kids chattered excitedly about their Christmas gifts, the winter dance, and the chance of a snowstorm in the coming days. The chill from outside clung to their coats as they removed their winter gear and stuffed them in their lockers. A lady in the front office told Nova her home-room teacher would assign her a locker.

Beads of sweat erupted on her forehead, and she wished she, too, could shed her coat. She knew it wasn't the heavy jacket causing damp tendrils of hair to cling to her face, though.

It was fear.

An old-fashioned bell rang with an ear-splitting trill as she entered the classroom. It sounded nothing like the modern buzz that signaled the start of each period at her former school. The school she loved, where she walked with confidence through the crowded halls, her best friend Ceci by her side. It was the only school she'd known before now—one where she knew everyone and offered a kind smile to the new kids, never realizing how frightened they might be. Now she was that new kid. And this morning, no kind smiles greeted her, only curious glances and whispers.

Nova tensed as she tried to make herself smaller, less noticeable. The room fell silent as the final note of the bell echoed through the empty halls before ending as abruptly as it began. There was only one empty desk in the quiet room. The teacher nodded at Nova and pointed to the seat.

This teacher must be strict, Nova thought as she made her way to the open seat. The students sat silently; there were no requests for everyone to quiet down, as was often the case when the first bell rang at her former school. She sat with her eyes cast down, fearful the teacher, Mrs. Parks, would call her up for a public introduction. There was no way she would be able to stand in front of all these strangers and talk about herself without trembling with nervous energy. Her voice would likely crack, making it sound as if she were fighting back tears. Thankfully, Mrs. Parks didn't have time for such introductions.

"We have a new student today," Mrs. Parks said, rising from her chair and moving to stand in front of Nova's desk. "Nova Eckley. Let's all welcome Nova and show her our hospitable Panther Pride." The teacher laid an index card on Nova's desk and lowered her voice to a whisper. "Here's your locker number and combination. The locker is right outside the classroom. You can go find it and put your belongings away."

Nova replied with a grateful smile and a nod. She took the card and made her way to the hallway, sensing twenty sets of eyes burrowing into her back as she moved toward the door.

"Alright then, you should be ready to turn in the first draft of your book report today," Mrs. Parks said in a booming voice as the door closed behind Nova.

There was no one in the hall. Nova's footfalls echoed through the corridor as she searched for and found the locker number on the card. As she slowly turned the dial on the lock, she heard a voice behind her.

"I've been waiting for you," the voice said in a whisper so soft Nova doubted she heard it. But she spun around looking for the person. The hall was still empty. She glanced in both directions, looking for a door shutting behind the unknown speaker, but saw nothing. With a shrug, she went back to the lock. As she lifted the handle and the locker popped open, she heard someone speak again.

"I've waited so long."

An icy chill wrapped itself around Nova as she turned abruptly, hoping to catch whoever was playing this joke on her. Again, there was no motion in the hall. She was definitely alone. Frightened now, she hurriedly removed her coat, stuffing it and her lunchbox into the locker before slamming it shut. She wanted out of this space and was now eager to get back to the classroom full of strangers.

When she returned to Room 215, she could see the teacher through a long narrow window that ran down the side of the door, strolling casually up and down the rows of desks. She grabbed the handle to the door and tried to yank it open, but it wouldn't budge. For a brief moment, she believed the teacher had locked her out of the class and felt hot tears building in her eyes, threatening to spill down her face.

Another cold wave of air rushed over her, and Nova had the sensation someone was standing behind her. She was too terrified to turn her head. Her body trembled, and she blinked hard, partly to fight back the tears and partly because she didn't want to see anything. Again, she tugged helplessly on the door. It wouldn't give. Reluctantly she opened her eyes and realized that no one in the class had noticed her struggles on the other side of the door.

Then she heard the voice again. This time, the person who spoke to her was so close that her hair moved with the force of the hidden person's breath.

"Help me."

Nova suppressed a scream. If she made the slightest sound, she was sure her homeroom classmates would notice her. The fear of making such a foolish first impression overpowered her fear of the invisible whispering, whatever it was. She tugged hard on the door, and this time, it opened easily—so easily she fought to compose herself so she wouldn't fall backward. She rushed to her desk, fearing her shaking legs would give out if she didn't sit down immediately.

For the remainder of the hour, Nova could not focus on the teacher's lecture. Terrifying thoughts swam to the surface of her mind, and she fought to push them back down. Was she hearing voices? Her father said he heard voices before he left his small family. Her dad's illness didn't rear its frightening and confusing head until he was a grown-up with a wife and a child. Nova had been told she was too young to be taken over by the overwhelmingly destructive traits of her father's disease. It was impossible.

She pushed these notions from her mind and vowed to never walk the hallways alone again.

Chapter 2

The morning passed by quickly. At the start of each new class, Nova sat holding her breath, hoping she wouldn't be put on the spot. No one spoke to her. Despite the crush of students surrounding her in the hall, Nova had never felt more alone.

At noon, she entered the lunchroom and was scared again by the blaring bell. *I wonder if I'll ever get used to that,* she thought. She scanned the room looking for a place to sit. The room was packed. Kids set their lunchboxes on the few remaining unoccupied chairs to save the seat next to them for their friends in the cafeteria line. One small table sat empty, crammed into the farthest corner of the room. Nova wound her way past the kids devouring their lunches, swiping their phone screens and talking loudly. She sat at the empty table and began to unpack her lunch.

A shadow slid over her. She froze, the realization hitting her that she would have to explain her celiac disease to a whole new group of people. At her old school, everyone knew she had celiac disease, and no one cared about it. She never felt like she was different. It was nice not having to detail the dos and don'ts of her dietary restrictions. Now she feared that the autoimmune disease would define her before someone got to know her without the gluten-free disclaimer. What if kids didn't accept her? Her heart ached for her elementary school.

"This seat open? Mind if I sit?"

Nova choked on her words when she heard this unexpected question.

"Um, no, yeah," she stammered. "I mean, yes, you can sit here."

She wrapped her arms around her lunch items, scooping them closer to her and making room for the shockingly tall boy to take a seat and set his lunch tray down. He looked uncomfortable at the small table. His long legs jutted out to the sides, and his elbows rested awkwardly on the tabletop.

"I'm Ayden," he said. "Ayden Simmons."

He fell silent, and Nova sat with a protein bar clenched in her hand, raised almost to her mouth when she realized the boy was waiting for a response. She froze, not giving her name, nor taking a bite from the bar.

"Hi, Ayden! Nice to meet you," he said. "My name is…"

Nova shook her head, trying to shake off the redness she felt erupting on her cheeks.

"Sorry, my name is Nova," she managed to eke out the words. "Nova Eckley."

"Nova? Cool name," Ayden replied. "You new here?"

"Yeah, this is my first day."

"Oooh, sorry, bummer. I know how you feel. We moved here in November. Bet I can one-up you though. You know what's worse than being the new kid?" He didn't wait for Nova's reply. "Being the new vice principal's kid.

Double whammy. Not many kids are down with being friends with the VP's son."

"Oh, well, if I'd had all the details on this seating arrangement before agreeing to it, I might've asked you to move on." Nova chuckled, feeling happy that Ayden made her feel more at ease than she had in a long time.

"Harsh, especially for someone sitting alone at the corner table," he shot back.

He didn't have to tell her he was kidding.

"I deserved that," she replied, her smile widening.

"Well, it is nice to meet you, Nova. And I should tell you, I don't go on recon missions for my mom. Your secrets are safe with me, should you choose to divulge them."

"Good to know," she replied, finally taking a bite of the protein bar.

As Ayden picked at the assortment of food on his tray, he eyeballed Nova and her lunch.

"Don't take this the wrong way," he started. "But that's a pretty nontraditional spread you got there—protein bar, grapes, carrot sticks … And what's that?"

"Hummus," she said quietly.

"Oh, you don't see too many kids with such a sophisticated palate these days."

"Yeah, I have celiac disease, which is a dire way of saying I can't eat gluten."

"I've heard of that. Think I have a cousin or something who has it," he said. His voice sounded muffled and hard to understand as he crammed a bread stick in his mouth. "That kind of sucks for you, though. Sorry."

"No need to apologize, but yeah, it does kind of suck sometimes."

"Well, if it makes you feel better, I'm allergic to shellfish. I can't go to seafood restaurants, so we're kind of even."

"Um, no, not even close. There are only like five restaurants I can eat at, and this town only has two of them, so…"

"Okay, you got me there. But does your skin explode in hives, and does your tongue swell like a balloon?" he asked.

"No, not exactly. My reaction to gluten isn't deadly, but it is pretty gross."

"Spare me the details," he replied. "It's hard enough to stomach this slop."

Her laugh cut off abruptly when she noticed the look on Ayden's face. It was an expression that said he'd offended someone. He dropped his eyes to his tray, shuffling tater tots around.

"Nova Eckley?" a voice boomed from behind her. She turned and found herself staring at a stained apron Her eyes trailed up the fabric, past a name tag that clung to a strap, until her gaze settled on a stern face framed by a mass of unruly gray hair trying to fight its way out of a hairnet.

"I heard that, Simmons," the woman said. "You don't like the grub? Bring your own."

The woman didn't wait for a reply.

"You Nova Eckley?" she asked.

"Um, yes, that's me," Nova stammered. The woman made her nervous for reasons she couldn't quite figure out.

"I got a notice from the office that you have some food intolerance or such. Can't remember the name, but you can't eat bread?"

"Yes, Ms.—?"

"Kids call me Mel." She pointed at the name tag. "No formalities. Ms. Melowski is too much of a mouthful. I've been Mel since I went to school here many moons ago."

Mel hadn't looked up from her clipboard for the entire conversation. She busied herself ticking off items on a list.

When finished, she tucked her pen behind her ear but still didn't look up.

"Yes, Mel." Nova found it difficult to address an adult in a school in such a casual manner. "I have celiac disease. I can't eat anything with wheat, barley, or rye in it."

Mel finally looked up from her clipboard and eyed Nova over her glasses, one eyebrow lifted questioningly like she'd been told an epic lie.

"Wheat?" she said, dropping the clipboard to her side and shifting her weight. She didn't bother trying to conceal her eye roll. "How exactly am I supposed to feed a kid who can't eat wheat?"

Nova got the feeling Mel was not directing this question toward her. Before she could reply, the woman continued.

"Now I think I've seen it all. I've had to cut out peanut butter and red dye, not as easy as you might think it is. I've got kids who can't eat eggs or milk products."

"Shellfish," Ayden boldly chimed in.

"Shellfish," she said, glancing at Ayden. Her expression softened considerably as if she were glad someone agreed with her and understood the challenges her job presented. Nova turned her head to Ayden, widening her eyes and pursing her lips.

"Seems like there's something new added to the list every year, but this one, I think this one takes the cake."

"Gluten-free cake," Ayden retorted.

Nova couldn't believe the boy's audacity.

"Gluten-free," Mel mumbled under her breath, followed by a tsk.

"Um, yeah, so I can't eat gluten, but it's no big deal. I never eat the school lunch. I always bring my own." Nova wanted this conversation to end.

"Always?" Mel questioned. "I've seen a fair share of

kids in my day who say they bring their lunches, but you know what?"

Nova had no idea what the question meant or if Mel wanted a reply, so she shook her head and stole another glance in Ayden's direction. His attention was again on his tray, where he was drawing smiley faces in a blob of ketchup.

"Then comes the day when that lunch box is forgotten. And you know who they come crying to when that happens?"

"You?" Nova hazarded a guess.

"Bingo! Me!" Mel replied. "I like you two. You seem to get it."

Ayden finished his ketchup art and looked up. A smile spread wide across his face as he nodded his head with enthusiasm before licking the ketchup off his finger.

"Well, Mel," Nova began. "I keep a stash of protein bars in my backpack just in case."

"So what you're saying is, I don't need to jump through impossible hoops to keep you nourished?"

"That's right. I rely on my mom and myself to keep me fed."

"Well, alrighty then. Guess that settles it. Welcome to Westland Park Middle School."

Mel turned her attention back to her clipboard. Nova watched as the woman walked back toward the lunch line.

"Did you get the impression that was the most unwelcoming welcome ever?" Ayden whispered, leaning across the table.

Before she could agree, the school bell screamed, letting everyone within a two-mile radius know the lunch break was over.

"Still haven't gotten used to that bell," Ayden said as he

got up with his tray. "Maybe we'll have a class together this afternoon."

"Maybe!" she said, as she stuffed things back into her bag.

Ayden smiled and walked to the line where kids returned their utensils and trays.

As Nova watched him, she was struck by how he towered over the other kids in line. She noted his slightly hunched posture. Even if he hadn't been the tallest boy in the school, he'd still stand out. He had long, shiny black hair and was lanky. When he stepped out of line, empty-handed, he looked back at Nova and gave her a wave. Her cheeks flushed, and she waved back in hopes of concealing her embarrassment that he'd caught her staring.

Ayden was in two of her afternoon classes. He spotted her as she shyly entered the classroom and waved her over to sit next to him. Her last class was choir, and she saw Ayden standing on the back riser the moment she entered the room. He was an alto and a giant, so he stood in the back on the top row, while she was on the bottom riser with the sopranos. She was comforted just knowing he was in the room with her. She was so grateful she had made a friend the first day; it made the changes easier to handle. They might be outsiders, but they were outsiders who had each other.

<hr>

Chapter 3

<hr>

Nova had to ride the bus home and naturally wished Ayden rode the same one. She sat alone near the back while students trickled in alone or in small groups. Through the window, she saw Ayden talking to a woman whom she recognized from the office that morning. The woman was most certainly his mom; she had the same sleek black hair he did, only hers was cut in an angled bob. The two spoke casually before hugging. Ayden held a skateboard that he tossed to the ground. He hopped on the board with practiced ease and glided down the sidewalk away from the school. She watched him until he disappeared around a corner.

As she leaned back in her seat, shoulders slumped, fidgeting with thread on her sweater, a student approached. Sensing a presence, Nova straightened her spine and glanced up with a smile, hopeful that maybe this girl would ask to sit next to her. She would love to have a friend on the bus. She and Ceci used to ride the same bus, and she remembered how long and boring those rides home were on the days when Ceci was absent from school.

"I'll let it slide this time, you being the new kid and all. But members of the concert choir sit in the back three rows, so you'll need to move." The girl, whom Nova recognized from her choir class, stood over Nova, tapping her foot, arms crossed, eyes fixed in a cold glare.

"I'm sorry?" Nova said, not apologetically, but in a way that told the girl she didn't understand.

"You need to move," the girl said more forcefully this time. "Concert choir kids sit back here and practice our vocals."

Several kids stood behind the girl, whose blonde hair was tied in a neat, slick ponytail. Her crystal blue eyes bore into Nova. As the girl scoffed loudly, Nova rose and grabbed her backpack, pushing past the group of kids and apologizing again. No one spoke to her. She scoured the bus and found the only empty spot was directly behind the bus driver. Tossing her bag down on the bench, she sat and slid to the window. There, she rested her head against the cold glass and listened to snippets of the conversations swirling behind her. Suddenly her backpack was pushed against her thigh, and she felt the pressure of another person sitting next to her. Her heart fluttered with a touch of gratitude that she might have a friend on the bus after all. She turned to greet the student.

But the seat was empty.

A chill settled upon her that didn't come from the open bus door. The cushion beside her was visibly indented as if an invisible person were sitting there. She pressed herself tightly against the wall of the bus and pulled her coat hood up, blocking her peripheral sight.

"Everybody take your seats and let's get rolling," the elderly bus driver yelled, his voice so heavy it silenced all the chatter momentarily. He pulled the handle and closed the door, and the bus slowly rolled out of the roundabout.

To avoid the icy spot next to her, Nova focused on the world outside. An unfamiliar landscape of strip malls, apartment complexes, grocery stores, and used car dealerships blurred by. Each time the bus lurched to a stop, she refused to glance to see who departed. She wasn't sure how many stops the bus made, but she soon saw her apartment complex and a wave of relief washed over her.

She jumped up and grabbed her bag, eager to get off the bus and away from the wraith-like occupant sharing her seat. Feeling a bit more courageous now, she glanced back to see the only other passenger on the bus was the girl who made her move from her chosen spot. The girl was engrossed in something on her phone when suddenly her head jerked back forcefully as if someone had tugged hard on her perfect ponytail.

"Ouch!" the girl hissed. She looked around her. She rubbed her head as she stood up, peering over the back of the seat searching for the culprit. Finding no one to blame, she rubbed her head some more as she went back to what she had been doing on her phone.

Nova quickly departed the bus, checked both ways for traffic, and hurried across the street. As she walked through the covered sidewalks of the complex, her mind spun with confusion and fear. She found her apartment, no small task since there were rows upon rows of identical buildings, and every door looked just like the next one. She unlocked the door, entered the tiny living room, and leaned back against the door after locking the deadbolt and sliding the chain back into place.

The school day had left her exhausted. If she lay down, she knew she'd be out in minutes. But her mother depended on her to get chores done and tend to herself. Her mom wouldn't be home until past Nova's bedtime, as she had taken a job working four ten-hour days a week at a nursing home. They both conceded the hours weren't ideal, but Mom needed a job quickly. Jobs in her field were sparse, and aside from the long hours, it fit her needs. Plus, Nova's grandmother lived at the nursing home. Her failing health had forced her into the facility, which was the reason Nova's mom made the decision to return to her hometown. Mom's plan was to pick up any other shifts she could, covering for people who needed time off, which meant she might not be around much. The first day of coming home to an empty house was tough. Knowing it was the first of many was too much for Nova to think about.

The apartment was eerily quiet, but faint noises from surrounding units echoed softly through the walls. Unnerved by the ghostly sounds, she flipped the television on and went to her room to remove her shoes and coat. Cheesy music filled the space, followed by a cheering audience and a flamboyant host. She recognized him from one of the lame game shows her grandmother liked to watch. Grateful the noise pushed away the loneliness, she went to the kitchen for a snack.

Held to the fridge by a magnet, Nova found a note her mother left her.

Welcome home!

I hope the day treated you well, and I can't wait to hear all the stories about your new adventure! I bought some frozen meals to make things easy since it was the first day for both of us. You get first pick since I won't be home before you go to bed.

I know it might be a little chilly in here, but please leave the thermostat where it is. Every penny counts. If you get too cold, bundle up.

I trust you locked the doors behind you when you got home, but make sure to undo the chain lock before you go to bed so I'm not locked out. Don't stay up too late!

Have a good night and know that I am missing you.

You are my world!

Mom

Nova couldn't help but smile while reading the note. But it also made her sad. Her mother never had to worry about where the thermostat was set before they moved here. She'd always been at home to greet Nova after school and take her to soccer practice or dance class. Frozen meals were a rare choice back then as her mother loved to cook and made delicious meals that she, her mother, and her father ate as they sat around their small dining room table in their tidy home and discussed the day's events.

That dreamy life she took for granted started to crumble slowly, as her dad's entire personality changed. It fell apart when he was diagnosed with schizophrenia. Nova didn't know much about the mental illness that had such a long and menacing name, but she did know it turned her dad into something she didn't recognize. Her mother cried every day as she struggled to keep his medications balanced.

One morning, Nova woke to find her mother crying on the floor. It took some time for her to get the words out to tell Nova that Dad was gone. He said he didn't like taking the medications, didn't like the way they made him feel. Seeing himself as a burden, he thought his wife and child were better off without him. Mom said he begged her to let him go and to not look for him. Nova was surprised her mother agreed to his request. Her mom tried to explain it to her, but in the end, all she could say was it was impossible to explain something to Nova that she herself couldn't understand.

Since that conversation, the two hadn't spoken much about her dad. Nova always believed someday he would return to them. He would miss them as much as she missed him and would come back.

Her mother sold their house, the one that sat across the street from Ceci's house, and moved them here. It all happened so fast. One day she was playing board games on a Friday night with her parents and Ceci; the next she was sleeping in a tiny room and walking into a new school where weird things plagued her already.

She went about her nightly routine, slid the chain lock open, got into bed, and cried herself to sleep.

Chapter 4

Two weeks flew by. Nova and Ayden became inseparable. The other students did not attempt to join their circle of two, and that was fine with both of them. They made each other laugh, and although it was unspoken, their friendship softened the blow of being the new kids who nobody else made room for. Becoming best friends with a boy was a little weird. Unlike her bond with Ceci, there were no sleepovers, no exchanging clothes or jewelry. She did Face-Time Ceci almost daily, which helped.

Nova didn't speak of it to anyone, not even her mom or Ayden, but she continued to be bothered by a feeling someone was always watching her when she was at school. Although she never saw anyone, she couldn't shake the notion someone was studying her. So far, she was successful at avoiding being alone in the school hallways or bathrooms, so no one could bother her. But she wasn't sure how long her lucky streak would last.

A soprano spot in the concert choir opened up when one of the members moved away. Mrs. Hastings suggested

Nova audition for the seat, and she jumped at the chance. Nova loved to sing, and while choir class was one of her favorites, she longed for more musical opportunities. Her stomach flip-flopped and her hands shook as she adjusted the microphone that stood like a lonely tree in the middle of the empty stage. The lights shone in her eyes so much that she couldn't make out who sat in the auditorium seats.

"Are you ready, Nova?" Mrs. Hastings shouted.

Nova took a deep breath and nodded. She reminded herself Ayden was in the audience for moral support, and that helped her relax a bit.

Mrs. Hastings counted her down and started playing the piano that sat just below and to the right of the stage. Despite hand-shaking nerves, Nova belted out the song beautifully when suddenly the music came to an abrupt stop. Not expecting this, Nova continued to sing in a strong voice for several beats before realizing she was singing without accompaniment. Her stomach flip-flopped, and she wondered if Mrs. Hastings was testing her. Maybe the teacher wanted to hear her sing acapella. Under this new pressure her confidence waned, her voice faltered and fell silent. From the audience, she heard the familiar snickering of some of the kids on her bus when someone said, "Awkward."

She knew the word came from shiny-ponytail girl, who she now knew as Caitlyn Rogers. Heat rose in Nova's face, and she fought back tears. It had taken all her courage to audition for the spot, and now it was going off the rails. She considered backing off the stage and hiding in the thick velvet curtains when Mrs. Hastings suddenly spoke.

"Who is walking around backstage?" the teacher asked no one in particular. "Did you see that? Ayden, did you see a shadow behind the scrim curtain?"

Some of the tension eased in Nova's stance as she realized it wasn't a mistake in her singing that caused Mrs. Hastings to pause. She peered over her shoulder and saw the shadow Mrs. Hastings spoke of. It stood almost directly behind Nova, motionless.

"I'll go check it out," Ayden said as he jumped up to the stage and gave Nova a shrug. Ayden sprinted toward stage left, and the shadow behind the curtain vanished. It didn't run or lay down; it simply evaporated as if it had never been there. Ayden didn't see this shadowy disappearing act, as he was behind the curtains calling out.

"Hey, who's back here? We're holding auditions, you know? You shouldn't be backstage."

There was no answer, just the subdued snickering of the concert choir kids led by Caitlyn.

"Quiet!" Mrs. Hastings demanded.

The laughter ended sharply. Ayden emerged from the wings of the stage and hopped down.

"There's no one there, Mrs. Hastings."

"Odd," Mrs. Hastings said in a tone that implied she didn't quite believe the boy. "I'm sorry, Nova. Can we take it from the top?"

Nova nodded and took a deep breath. When she sang the final note, she couldn't hide the smile on her face. She was confident she sang better than ever for this audition.

"Nicely done, Nova!" Mrs. Hastings exclaimed. "I think we've found the newest member of the Woodland Park Concert Choir."

One person in the audience clapped wildly and whistled before shouting for an encore. She knew it was Ayden, her only supporter. The clapping continued and Ayden let out a "Woohoo!"

"That's enough, Ayden," Mrs. Hastings said with a chuckle. "Welcome to the team, Nova!"

At the back of the auditorium, a shaft of light flashed

as a door opened and several kids left. Nova spotted Caitlyn, as she was the last of the group to exit. Before letting the door close behind her, Caitlyn turned and eyed Nova. For a moment Nova was certain Caitlyn would speak, and she held her breath, hoping but doubting the girl would say something encouraging. Instead, Caitlyn let out an audible scoff, and the door closed slowly behind her, shrouding the seats in darkness again.

Nova walked off stage to grab her backpack. As she approached the curtains she saw the shadow. It stood behind the scrim curtain; and while it appeared that the person was clapping, the sound of the applause didn't reach Nova's ears. There was absolute silence backstage. Nova tried to build the courage to approach the shadow, but when she pulled the curtain aside, the shadow faded away. The only thing left was an icy chill that penetrated the warm glow of the stage lights. Nova shivered, a puff of vapor escaped her lips. She turned quickly and walked away, looking over her shoulder as she went.

Telling herself that it was nothing and to chill, Nova hopped down from the stage and joined Ayden in the audience.

"You really think I did well?" she asked, knowing what the answer was.

"You sang your heart out," Ayden replied. "You sounded a million times better than the self-proclaimed queen of concert choir."

"Queen of concert choir?"

"Caitlyn Rogers, dork."

"Oh, yeah, Caitlyn. I don't know if I'm a better singer than Caitlyn..." Nova trailed off.

"Right, stay humble," he said. "Get over yourself. That girl has been taking private voice lessons since she was five years old. She let that little fact slip one day. How many private vocal coaches have you had?"

"Um, none," Nova replied, glancing at her friend.

"Well, it's obvious you've got Caitlyn Rogers on edge. She's not used to being challenged. I hear the stories from my mom."

The two grabbed their backpacks from the bleacher chairs and said goodbye to Mrs. Hastings. As they exited the dark auditorium and walked into the sunlit hall, they shielded their eyes. The hall stood empty, as the audition took place immediately after school.

"Speaking of my mom," Ayden said, "we better hustle out to her car. She doesn't like to be left waiting."

"It was nice of her to give me a ride," Nova said, trying to keep up with her long-legged friend.

"Oh, that's not all. When she found out that you eat dinner alone most nights, she insisted you eat at our house tonight."

"Oh, um, that's kind of hard for me, with the celiac and all."

She hated having to explain why she couldn't just sit down and eat a meal someone had prepared. Despite knowing most people understood, she always felt like she came off as rude or unappreciative.

"You don't know my mom very well," Ayden said. "She's been researching gluten-free meals ever since I asked her to give you a ride. She's got it all planned out, a one-hundred-percent gluten-free meal. Last night she searched every bottle on her spice shelf to make sure nothing had gluten. She's using disposable utensils and a throwaway roasting pan. I guarantee you will not get sick. I had to disinfect the entire kitchen and make sure there wasn't a morsel of gluten hiding anywhere. Is that the right word, morsel? I don't know, but she's gone to great lengths to make sure you can eat this meal without fear."

Still apprehensive, Nova smiled.

"My mom would die before she got you sick."

———————————————

Chapter 5

———————————————

Ayden wasn't faking when he said his mother was abundantly cautious. In the Simmons's kitchen, Mrs. Simmons had Nova inspect every ingredient of the dish she prepared. Nova felt a little embarrassed but grateful for the effort. The only other home she had ever felt comfortable eating in was Ceci's.

Once Nova gave the green light to Mrs. Simmons, the woman shooed them out of the kitchen.

"You two go find something to do while I cook. Go watch some TV or play some video games," she said, putting an apron on. "We'll eat as soon as your dad gets home."

"Whatcha wanna do?" Ayden asked as they entered the living room.

"I don't know … That porch swing looks pretty fun," she replied. "I've never actually swung in one."

"Well, not sure you've been missing anything, but sure, let's go have a swing."

He opened the front door and motioned for Nova to have a seat on the bright red swing. The two pushed off, and the swing rocked slowly back and forth. They were silent for a while, watching a woman bundled up in layers walking a small dog dressed in a Sherpa coat. Some younger kids rode by on bicycles, waving to the two teens on the swing.

"Oh, I almost forgot my laundry!" Ayden exclaimed. "Stay here, I'll be right back. I need to move my laundry into the dryer. My mom hates it when I leave my clothes in the washer. Think I'll check on Mom too and make sure she isn't overwhelmed in her role as gluten-free chef."

Nova laughed. "I never meant to be a burden."

"I'm kidding. My mom loves these kinds of challenges. I'm sure she is doing fine."

Ayden entered the house, leaving Nova swinging alone in the red chair. She closed her eyes and breathed in crisp air that warned of coming snow. As she swayed slowly, she heard someone knocking on the window next to her. She looked up, expecting to see Ayden making faces or smooshing his face against the glass. Her feet hit the ground, stopping the momentum of the swing in an instant.

It wasn't Ayden peering at her from the window, but a girl.

The girl looked nearly transparent and seemed to float in an ethereal motion that defied gravity, like the flickering flame of a candle. That wasn't the only thing different about the girl, either. Her clothes, while gray and wispy, were not like Nova's. She had a sweater vest over a button-up shirt and wore a plaid, pleated skirt. Her attire was nothing like what Nova would expect to see a girl her age wearing. The girl's hair was parted down the middle and held tightly back by barrettes on each side of her head. Although Nova couldn't see tears coming from the girl, she looked dismal. Nova had never seen a person look more sad.

The girl didn't scare her, but her mind grasped for explanations for the strange apparition-like figure being in Ayden's house. He had never mentioned a little sister. And if he had, she was sure it wouldn't be a swaying ghostly girl in old-fashioned clothes who appeared to be almost trapped behind the window. Before her mind could dive deeper for an explanation, the girl put her hand out and touched the window. Nova couldn't understand why, but she was compelled to rise from the swing and make her way toward the girl. The girl did not withdraw, but instead, something in her eyes called for Nova to hurry.

Nova stood close to the girl and raised her hand to the window. The two would be touching if it weren't for the thin panel of glass that separated them. The spot on the windowpane where the girl's hand rested was so cold, Nova felt the burning shock of an icy blast from it. Still, she did not move her hand away. The girl stared Nova directly in the eyes, her expression pleading as she mouthed something. While Nova couldn't hear what the girl said, she easily read her lips.

"Help me."

Nova wasn't sure how long the two stood staring at each other. The trance was broken when Ayden emerged noisily from the house.

"It's starting to smell pretty good in there. It's making my stomach growl. Shh! Can you hear it?"

The door slammed loudly, and in an instant, the girl was gone. Nova didn't move.

"Whatcha doing there, Nova?" Ayden questioned.

Nova didn't reply.

"You okay?"

"Oh, um yeah. Sorry. I just…" She didn't know what

to say. She looked at the hand she had raised to the window and was surprised to see her palm was an angry red, just as it looked when she made snowballs without gloves on. She tucked the hand under her arm and the chill burned through her heavy sweater.

"I think I saw my dad pulling up. Just in time! I'm so hungry I could eat a gluten-free meal," he joked.

"Nice one," Nova replied with a smirk. "Hey, you don't think your house is haunted or anything, do you?" She tried to make the question sound casual but could tell by Ayden's face that she hadn't succeeded.

"Haunted? Um, why the whacky talk?"

"Oh, I don't know. It seems kind of old and maybe a tiny bit spooky, the kind of house that might be haunted, you know?"

"Well, hate to burst your eerie little bubble, but no, I have not met anyone lurking about in a white sheet. There is a pet cemetery out back which is a little creepy, but there's only like one animal buried there. We found a flat headstone of sorts. It has a little dog face, and there's a name on it too. It was like Okra or something. But we haven't seen ghostly, muddy paw prints or anything. We haven't lived here long, though, so who knows."

"Dinner!" Mrs. Simmons hollered from the kitchen, breaking the discomfort of the conversation to Nova's relief.

"Here goes nothing," Ayden said, opening the door for her.

As she moved past her friend, she glanced back at the window, half expecting to see the girl again. She was no longer there, but a frosty imprint remained on the glass in the shape of a hand.

———

Nova wished her mom was home when Mrs. Simmons dropped her at their apartment. There were so many things she wanted to share. What started as her best day since moving crumbled into a scary, troubling evening. As she entered the dark, lonely apartment, shadows slipped into the corners of the living room and ducked behind the furniture. Every sound caused her to jump, pause what she was doing, and search for the source. She turned the television on, cranked the volume higher than necessary, and flipped on every light in the small apartment. These measures helped a little, but she was still on edge.

Disembodied voices, visions of a ghostly form—was she hallucinating? She didn't know what scared her more —that she could have inherited her father's condition, or that she was being haunted by an actual spirit. Both options were terrifying and left her feeling helpless. She had never wanted a hug from her mom more.

She tried to FaceTime Ceci, but her friend wasn't available. A call to Ayden after just leaving his house might be weird. So she resorted to watching YouTube videos. The distraction did little to quiet her fears.

She went about her nightly routine, her mind grappling with dreadful thoughts. While she brushed her teeth, she studied her face in the mirror. Despite being frightened, she didn't have the same look in her eyes that her father had when he began to unravel. She had her father's green eyes, everyone said so. But before her dad left, his eyes conveyed broken darkness.

Turning off the lights was something she couldn't bring herself to do. Her mom would be mad, no doubt, and would be worried about the electric bill. She'd have to come clean with her mom and tell her she got spooked and needed the lights on to make her feel safer. If her mom was really mad, Nova might have to use tears and push her mom's buttons a bit, make her feel guilty for leaving Nova alone so much. Nova didn't want to do that to her mom, but she couldn't deny that adjusting to being a latchkey kid was challenging, especially since she was an only child and new to town.

She found it difficult to fall asleep that night. But she heard her mother slip in quietly. Her mom moved around the apartment, getting something to eat, and perhaps looking through the mail. Finally, Nova heard the sound she'd been waiting to hear. Her nightly signal that all was safe because she was no longer alone. A squeaky floorboard sat outside the bathroom door in the hallway separating her mother's room from her own. Mom joked that a feather dropping on the old, creaky hardwood would make the boards moan in protest. Most nights, Nova was asleep by the time her mom got home from work. While her mother did her best to be quiet as a mouse, she couldn't avoid summoning a cry from the floor. The sound always stirred Nova from her sleep, then sent her into heavier slumber by casting out the loneliness.

As badly as she wanted to share the day's events with her mom, she couldn't drag herself out of bed. Her eyelids grew heavy and sleep finally found her. She could talk to Mom tomorrow evening, as she would have a night off.

Chapter 6

The next day as Nova made her way across the crowded lunchroom to the table she and Ayden claimed as their outcast spot, a voice stopped Nova in her tracks.

"Hey, new girl," the voice said, rising above the clamor of commotion in the room.

Even though she'd been there for a few weeks, Nova knew they were talking to her and was surprised to see Caitlyn was the one who called out to her. Caitlyn knew Nova's name by now. It irked Nova that she continued to call her 'new kid.'

"Since you are in concert choir now, I guess you've earned a seat at this table," Caitlyn said.

"Come on over. We'll make room," said a boy sitting next to Caitlyn as he edged closer to the popular blond, making space on the bench.

"I, um—" Nova stuttered, her eyes scanning the room for Ayden. He wasn't at their usual table, and she didn't see him in the cafeteria line. Maybe he was absent today. "Okay," she replied, her head swimming with doubt and trepidation.

Nova slid in between the boy whose name she didn't know and another girl she only recognized from concert choir. Sweat beads sprung up on her forehead as she unpacked her lunch bag. She believed rightfully that all eyes at the table were focused on her as she removed her food.

"What's that?" a girl sitting across from her said. The girl had bouncy, red curls and a splatter of freckles across her nose.

"Um, it's hummus," Nova replied quietly.

"Hummus?" Caitlyn replied, an air of disgust in her tone. "Why would you bring hummus in your lunch? It looks kind of gross. What else do you have in there? A protein bar. Some weird-looking crackers. Are you on some strange diet?"

"Well, see, I, um, have..." Nova struggled with her words. "I have celiac disease. I can't eat gluten."

"Oh," the boy next to her chimed in. "My mom went gluten-free. She says gluten makes her bloated."

"Eww, don't talk like that while I'm eating," the redhead replied.

"What does that mean, even?" Caitlyn asked in a snooty tone.

"Well, I can't eat things like most bread and pasta, cakes and cookies," Nova tried explaining. "Well, unless they are gluten-free. It's basically wheat, rye, and barley products. It's kind of weird."

"Sounds weird," retorted the red-haired girl.

Don't be so rude, Ainsley," Caitlyn replied.

"I wasn't being rude. It's crazy to think you can't eat pasta. I'd die!"

Nova wished the ground would open and swallow her when there was a shift in the conversation.

Caitlyn asked, "Do you know everyone's names?"

"Not really," Nova replied, grateful the gluten conversation had ended.

"This is Jamison; he's our star baritone." Caitlyn pointed to a boy sitting next to Ainsley. Jamison's skin could only be described as pasty, giving his pale skin a mottled look. He wore a constant pout and about two more layers of clothing than anyone needed despite winter's chill outside.

Nova felt an elbow jab her ribs as the girl sitting next to her leaned and didn't quite whisper, "He's a bit of a hypochondriac. If the temperature drops below forty degrees, his lips turn purple."

"I heard that, Layla," Jamison said, lobbing a cheese cube at the girl.

"And Tatum." Caitlyn pressed on without acknowledging the wee food fight. "His alto voice is as smooth as butter." Her voice took on a dreamlike quality as she gazed at the hulking boy. The others at the table let out a harmonious groan. Caitlyn brushed the boy's long brown curls from his shoulder. Tatum was so large he stood out among the other middle school boys. He had a chiseled chin and broad shoulders. Nova wondered if he'd been held back a year or even two.

Caitlyn rattled off a few more names: Layla who sat next to Nova, Tai, and Mateo. Nova smiled and nodded at each. Tai flashed her a peace sign, while Mateo ignored everyone over something on his phone.

Nova felt overwhelmed by the situation and allowed herself to briefly consider how different this lunch experience was from any other she'd had. She hoped her discomfort wasn't as obvious to the concert choir group as she felt it was. A change of subject drew her back into the fold of the conversation.

"So, are you going to audition for the solo in the spring

concert, Nova?" Caitlyn asked as she peeled the rind off a tangerine.

Taken aback by the swift change of topic, Nova swallowed hard and thought for a moment about how to reply.

"I didn't know there was a solo," she said, choking down a bite of food.

"Yes, Mrs. Hastings highlights some of the more gifted vocalists in the spring concert, but you have to try out for it. There's usually a boy solo and a girl solo. Of course, I am auditioning. Wondering who my competition might be this year." Caitlyn eyed each of the girls at the table, her gaze falling on Nova as she finished her statement.

"When are the auditions?" Nova asked.

"They should be coming up soon. Mrs. Hastings must not have thought you were up to the gig if she hasn't mentioned it to you yet. Even if you started now, you'd be rushed to prepare a piece. It's probably for the best. It'd be odd to have a brand-new student win the spot. I'm sure the pressure would be too much for you."

"I don't know. Maybe I could use a piece I'm familiar with."

"Suit yourself," Caitlyn said, distaste exposed in her expression. "I wouldn't get your hopes up, though. I've taken years of private voice lessons. I'm the obvious first choice." Caitlyn popped a wedge of the tangerine in her mouth. The other kids at the table nodded and murmured their agreement.

———

Ayden caught Nova's attention later that day and waved her over to his spot on the risers before class started.

"Didn't see you at lunch. Well, I saw you at lunch, but what were you doing at the mean girls' table?"

"Sorry, I didn't see you. It was all kinds of weird."

"I can imagine," Ayden said. "Oh, well, guess you won't have much use for me now since you're in with the 'it' crowd."

Nova believed he was joking, but sensed doubt in his voice.

"Oh, puh-lease! All they did was warn me that I shouldn't try out for a solo and made me feel like a freak for having an autoimmune disease. There were zero warm-fuzzy moments."

The tension left Ayden's shoulders and he smiled at her.

Mrs. Hastings clapped her hands signaling the start of class. Nova made her way to her spot on the risers, taking her place between Caitlyn and Ainsley.

The class passed by in its usual way. But as it grew to an end and the kids gathered their stuff, heading for the door, Mrs. Hastings called Nova over.

"Nova, can I have a word with you?"

Nova stopped and looked back at the teacher. She noticed Caitlyn and Ainsley pause at the door.

"Sure, Mrs. Hastings. What's up?"

Mrs. Hastings spotted two girls standing at the door, as well.

"Go on, girls. Class is over. I need a word with Nova."

Caitlyn and Ainsley left the room, but Nova saw them lingering in the hallway through the long narrow window at the side of the door.

"I wanted to see," Mrs. Hastings began, "if you would like to audition for a solo in the spring concert. I think your voice adds to the beauty of our work and would love to see you have the chance to stand out. What do you think?"

Nova's cheeks flushed an embarrassed crimson, but she eagerly accepted Mrs. Hastings's offer to audition. Despite having a conversation that lasted several minutes with her teacher, Nova saw the two girls just steps ahead of her as she left the choir classroom. The two were huddled in a conspiratorial discussion. Caitlyn looked back at Nova.

"Better hurry or you'll miss the bus, Nova."

Nova noted the time on a clock jutting out high on the hallway wall and picked up her pace. If she missed the bus, her mother would have to take off work to come get her. Mom sent her a text earlier that day apologizing for taking an additional shift but saying she would be home for dinner. She didn't want to jeopardize her mom's job, so her quick pace became a jog.

A wave of relief washed over her. The bus was still in the roundabout. Caitlyn and Ainsley were boarding, and Nova ran to make it to the bus before the door shut. She looked expectantly at the group in the back of the bus, wondering if they would extend an offer to sit with them on the bus as they had in the cafeteria. There was only one empty seat, and no one called her over. She took her place at the front, behind the driver.

The bus began to roll away and the familiar chill set upon Nova. Pressure next to her told her the unseen passenger was riding along as usual.

A steady rain began to fall as the bus lumbered through town, making its stops. The sky was gray and heavy and people on the streets popped open umbrellas or covered their heads with their bags.

When the bus rolled to a stop at Nova's apartment complex, the rain tapered off to a sprinkling drizzle. Nova didn't bother trying to cover her head, but as she made her way across the street, she looked back at the bus. She shook her head in disbelief as she glimpsed someone sitting in the very spot she just occupied. It was the girl, the girl she saw at Ayden's house. Again, the girl raised her hand to the window, but this time she wrote 'Help me' on the foggy windowpane.

45

Chapter 7

That night at dinner, her mom couldn't hide the weariness in her eyes. Nova spoke only of happy, "normal" things and didn't burden her mom with the fears that plagued her. No mention was made of the lights being on when she came home the night before. Nova spoke excitedly about concert choir and auditioning for a solo. She rattled on about Ayden and his mother's gluten-free meal and pushed the bad things out of her mind so that her voice projected a cheerful tone.

Mom used her fork to move green beans around her plate and gave Nova a tired smile.

"I'm so happy for you, Nova. I knew you'd make friends. You're a shoo-in for the solo. I could listen to your beautiful singing all day."

"Thanks, Mom," Nova said as she rose from the table. She planted a kiss on the top of her mom's head. "I'll clean up the dinner mess. Maybe you could go find a movie for us to watch."

"Are you sure you're feeling okay?" Mom joked as she got up and placed the back of her hand on Nova's forehead. "You don't feel feverish, but volunteering to clean up, that's so unlike you."

Nova pushed her mom's hand away with a giggle and an eye roll.

"I'm fine, Mom."

She took her mother's plate and went to the sink.

"Wanna watch something scary? A ghost story maybe?"

Nova almost dropped the plates at the mention of the word *ghost*. She shook her head and regained her composure.

"Nah, I think I'm in the mood for a comedy if that's okay with you," she replied.

"Comedy it is," Mom said, leaving the kitchen.

Nova jumped out of her skin and almost lost her grip on the casserole dish when her mom popped her head back in the kitchen.

"Ooh, sorry to scare you. I just wanted to tell you how proud I am of you. I know none of this stuff, first your dad and then the move, has been easy for you. You're such a trooper."

"Thanks, Mom," Nova said, placing the last dish in the dishwasher.

She and Mom watched a movie and laughed like they hadn't in a long time. About halfway through the movie, Nova noticed her mom wasn't cracking up over things that would normally cause her to snort-laugh. She looked over to see Mom had fallen asleep. Nova couldn't bring herself to wake her up, so she got the crocheted blanket her grandma made off the back of the recliner and tucked it around her mom. Then, she turned off the TV and lights and made her way to the bathroom to get ready for bed. The creaking board let out its jarring squeal, and Nova froze. Turning her head back toward the living room, she saw the noise hadn't woken her mom and let out a quiet sigh of relief.

Back in her bedroom, she FaceTimed Ceci. She needed to talk to someone about the weird things that were happening and didn't feel close enough yet to Ayden to tell him she was seeing and hearing things. Ceci would understand and wouldn't laugh or ridicule her.

She and Ceci loved scary movies and read every ghost story they could get their hands on. Nova loved the thrill of safe scares, the kind that resulted in peals of laughter once the movie ended. This, though, was different. Believing you were actually haunted was no fun at all. She took comfort in sensing the mysterious bus rider had never followed her home.

Unsure about how to start the discussion, she dove right in, not prepping her friend for the topic.

"So, some weird stuff has been happening to me at school," Nova started.

"Weird stuff? Like a cute guy crush? Secret admirer? Nova, spill!"

"I wish!" Nova replied. "No, this isn't good stuff. It's scary stuff and it's creeping me out."

Nova rehashed all the spooky things happening to her. The voice in the hall on her first day, the not-so-empty seat on the bus every afternoon, the shadowy figure on stage with her during her tryout, and the manifestation of a girl in the window—first at Ayden's and then again on the bus.

Ceci listened intently, never showing any sign she didn't believe her friend.

"Wow, that is creepy," Ceci finally said after Nova had spilled the details so quickly that she barely took a breath. "I think you know what you need to do, right?" she asked.

"Are you kidding me? I have no idea what to do. I just want it all to go away," Nova lamented.

"Well, yeah," Ceci said. "Going away would be nice, but it doesn't sound like burning some sage and telling her to go to the light is what's called for here."

"Yeah, pretty sure I'd get suspended for lighting up a sage bundle," Nova replied with a laugh. "So you have a plan for me that doesn't involve expulsion?"

"Yes, dufus! It's obvious. First, you need to find out who she is. Did someone die at the school? Maybe on the bus? Any ghost hunter worth their weight knows you have to find the source of the haunting."

"I wouldn't know where to begin. But I guess you're right."

"I'm always right, Nova!" Ceci said with a straight face. Her lips twitched as she fought off the smile giving her away, and she couldn't suppress her laughter any longer.

Chapter 8

Nova made her way through the throngs of students pouring into the cafeteria, her sights set on what she now considered to be *her* table—the one where she and Ayden were able to block out the din of lunchroom chaos and talk about anything and everything. Suddenly Caitlyn stepped in front of her. Nova almost ran into the girl.

"Hey, Nova, come sit with us today. I got you a surprise," Caitlyn said.

"Well, I…" Nova stammered. She saw Ayden sitting at their table, his brow knotted as he gingerly poked at the items on his lunch tray. He looked as if he were trying to determine what today's mystery entree might be. He didn't see Nova struggling to escape Caitlyn's invitation.

"Just come see," Caitlyn urged, her hand clasping Nova's elbow, guiding her toward the table reserved for the concert choir kids. "I think you'll like it!"

Nova gave in and allowed Caitlyn to lead her to the table where the group sat, always in the same seat, as if they'd been assigned.

"I found these while I was at the grocery store with my

mom," Caitlyn said. "I instantly thought of you and your food plight, so I insisted my mom get them."

Caitlyn pushed a brightly colored cookie package toward Nova. The brand was familiar; Nova had indulged in the pricey but delicious gluten-free cookies many times. They were even her favorite flavor, chocolate mint.

"I have to admit, I tried them myself," Caitlyn said. "And I must say, I was pleasantly surprised."

Tatum slid his hand toward the package, attempting to take one of the cookies for himself. Caitlyn caught the action out of the corner of her eye and slapped the boy's hand.

"Don't even think about it," she whispered through clenched teeth. "These things are triple the price of regular cookies!"

"Oh, wow, Caitlyn," Nova began. "I don't know what to say."

"For starters, thanks and may I have one, please," Caitlyn replied in a snarky tone.

"Right, yeah, thanks so much! These are my favorites." Nova took two cookies from the package and ate them quickly. "Wow, I've forgotten how good these are," she said with her mouth full of minty chocolate cream.

"Eat as many as you'd like," Caitlyn said. "It does my heart good to see you eat something normal after watching you suffer through hummus and weird-looking crackers every day."

Nova sat at the table for the remainder of the lunch period. As she packed the remnants of her lunch back into her lunch bag, she pulled another cookie out of the package. This time she took a minute to examine the cookie. The treat fell from her hand when she realized the logo stamped on the cookie itself was not the logo she was used to seeing. Before she could make the connections in her mind, she felt a hot flush work its way through her body, starting at her forehead and burning its way down to her toes. She recognized this sensation and knew what to expect next.

She doubled over as an intense cramp gripped her stomach. Panic overtook her as she grabbed her lunch bag and calculated how long it would take her to get to the bathroom closest to the cafeteria. Without saying a word to anyone, she bolted toward the cafeteria door.

"Walking feet, young lady!"

Nova ignored the shout from a teacher on lunch duty and picked up the pace as another cramp ripped through her midsection. A line of chattering girls spilled into the hallway from the girl's restroom. The bathroom was packed. She couldn't imagine the humiliation she would feel if she pushed her way through the crowd only to spill the contents of her stomach in one of the stalls of the crowded room. Or worse yet, if she didn't make it into a stall before tossing her proverbial and literal cookies. She ran past the closest restroom in a desperate search for another place to go, preferably one where she could be alone.

The cookies Caitlyn had given her were not gluten-free. Nova knew she had hours ahead of her that involved horrible stomach pains, dizziness, and vomiting that would culminate in a deep, but troubled sleep. After sleeping most of it off, she would face the hours-long headache from dehydration and the brain fog that could last days. Since her diagnosis, she'd been fortunate to only have consumed gluten accidentally a handful of times. The process of her body ridding itself of the offending protein was long and painful and grueling.

A cramp hit her hard, knocking the air out of her and stopping her in her tracks as she doubled over in agony.

She found herself at the entrance of a wing that was currently off-limits due to renovations. No workers were present at this time, and the corridor was dark. The only light trickled in faintly through the dirty windows high upon the wall. Skeletal scaffolds lined the hall, and dusty drop cloths lay draped over the floor. At the end of the long hall, she could make out a sign: 'Girl's Restroom.' She ducked under the caution tape and snaked her way through the scaffold beams. Leaping over a saw and other construction items, she made it to the bathroom door. Relief washed over her briefly, as the door gave way with a noisy creak. It wasn't locked and it was empty.

The bathroom was dark, its high windows even grimier than the ones in the hall. She groped for a light switch and flipped it on. A solitary fluorescent tube lit up while another flashed and tried unsuccessfully to sputter to life. A low, electric buzz emanated from the old fixtures. The bathroom and stall doors were the color of vanilla pudding, and the floors were cold orange tiles with filthy gray grout.

She rushed to the first stall door—it was locked. The next door wouldn't give either. Door after door was jammed shut, unwilling to open for her until she reached the last stall in the long line. A cry of gratification escaped her lips as the door slammed open. She fell to her knees. The contents of her stomach were purged in wave after wave of gut-twisting pain.

Chapter 9

She didn't know how long she had remained crouched on the bathroom floor. The shrill cry of the bell echoed in the hall outside. There was no way she could make it to class in this condition. She would have to wait it out, here on the cold floor, until she felt comfortable enough to get to the nurse's office.

After several minutes, she rose on shaky legs and made her way to the bank of sinks. Her reflection in the mirror frightened her. The dim room with a noisy flickering light couldn't conceal her ashen face. Under bloodshot eyes, deep gray bags made her look as if she'd missed days' worth of sleep. She turned the knob on the sink. A pipe in the wall banged loudly, causing her to jump. The faucet sputtered and spit out a rust-colored, coppery-smelling liquid before a clear stream of cooling water poured freely. She splashed it over her face.

Nausea gripped her stomach again, and she pushed back into the stall. She was powerless to control the gasping, choking dry gags. The sound of her struggles echoed through the empty bathroom. Eventually, she was able to regain some sense of control and fell back against the metal wall of the stall. Hot tears spilled from her eyes. Why would Caitlyn pull such a cruel prank on her? Were any of the other concert choir kids in on the dirty trick? The auditions for the solo were later that day. Had Caitlyn known Nova would have this intense reaction to the gluten? Was it her plan to make Nova so sick she'd miss her chance to win the coveted solo?

She wiped her mouth with her sweater and brushed the tears away. She needed to make her way to the nurse's office and feared how upset her mother would be for having to leave work to come get her.

She tried to rise on weak legs, when she heard the bathroom door squeak open, banging against the wall as if someone shoved it violently. She froze in a squatting position, wondering if it was Caitlyn or a teacher or a construction worker. She knew her voice didn't have the strength to explain why she was in this forgotten bathroom at the end of a closed-off corridor. An uncomfortable silence hung in the air after the door squealed slowly closed. Frozen in place, she waited for the person to speak. All she heard were footfalls, slowly making their way down the long aisle of stall doors.

A chill penetrated the room; her breath escaped in a vapor as she exhaled shallowly. Whoever entered the bathroom stopped directly in front of the stall where Nova cowered. She clenched her eyes closed, expecting someone to shove the door open or call out. She hadn't secured the latch on the stall, as she'd assumed she would be alone.

Time crawled to a stop as the person on the other side of the stall remained silent and motionless. She took two deep breaths and built the courage to speak.

"He– hello? Is someone out there?" she asked meekly.

Her question was followed by a long, nerve-shattering

silence. Then a sound found Nova's ears. It was the unmistakable, soft crying of a girl. After a few moments of listening to the sobs, Nova felt tears building in her own eyes. The weeping sounded haunting and desperate.

Suddenly, the lonely light snapped off with an electrical zap, throwing the entire bathroom into darkness. Nova's tears of concern for the person who stood on the other side of the metal barrier turned to fear. Inch by inch, Nova lowered her head to peek under the stall door. Her hands trembled, as she braced herself on the dingy floor. Her eyes adjusted to the murky haze, and she dropped low enough to see under the door. At the same time, the crier crouched, and Nova found herself face-to-face with a wispy presence. A strangled gasp erupted from deep in her throat. She clamored back toward the corner of the stall, behind the toilet, eyes clenched tightly.

"Help me," the girl on the floor whispered.

Nova needed to get out of this space. She bounded up and shoved the stall door open, ready to jump over the girl lying on the floor—but the girl was gone. She'd vanished. The wraith-like girl's sudden absence did nothing to calm Nova's terrified state. The door looked so far away as Nova bolted through the dark room. But soon it was within reach, and as her hand connected with the handle, she expected to burst into the hallway.

Instead, her body collided with the solid door. It was locked. How could that be? She'd come through it minutes ago, as had the now unseen girl. Nova pivoted in place, her eyes darted madly around the room, instinctively looking for another escape. A scream clawed its way up her throat. The girl was standing—standing right in front of her, close enough to touch.

The girl was no longer crying, but her expression conveyed sadness and helplessness. She screamed in Nova's face, and the energy from her wailing lifted Nova's hair off her shoulders. She turned her head to avert the icy blast of the girl's piercing screech. As quickly as it started, it stopped. The room was quiet again. Despite the silence and her tightly closed eyes, Nova felt the girl was still close. Slowly, she turned her head and allowed one eye to open. The girl remained there; again, she spoke.

"Please, help me," she pleaded before flickering in front of Nova's face and finally fading away before her eyes.

The temperature in the room climbed and the lights popped back on, one a solid beam of light, the other resuming its off-and-on twitch. Nova leaned against the bathroom door and almost fell as it gave way, releasing her from the confines of the restroom.

Now in the hallway, Nova forced the door closed and fell back against it, urging her pulse to slow and her breathing to calm. She scanned her surroundings in search of another place she could run to should her stomach revolt again. There were two trash bins, one halfway down the hall and the other at its mouth. Cautiously, she stepped forward to make her way back down the wing; her body pressed tightly to the side of the hall where the trash bins sat. She hated the thought of an unsuspecting construction worker coming upon a bin she had used as a barf bag, but there was no way she was going back into that bathroom. Her next stop was the nurse's office.

As she made her way toward the brightly lit foyer, she heard voices growing near and ducked behind a tower of plywood. Ms. Merritt rounded the corner with a man dressed in overalls and a hard hat.

"We're about ready to get started on this wing, Ms. Merritt," the man said. "We've been using it for storage mostly. We need to know what to do with the items in this trophy case, and then we can forge ahead."

"This is the original footprint of this entire school," Ms. Merritt spoke as she surveyed the hall. "I'd hoped we could close it off for good. It's ancient. The school board had other ideas, however."

"Well, ma'am, I'm certain we can make it shine again like it did back in its heyday."

Ms. Merritt's laughter echoed down the corridor.

"Oh, Ben, I wish you the best, but this old place is on its last leg. All the spackle in the world couldn't make this building look new again."

The man tapped the glass of the trophy case, drawing Ms. Merritt back to the subject matter that brought them down the dark corridor.

"Ah, yes, the panther. Well, of course, the panther stays. He's our school mascot after all. Maybe you could build a pedestal in the lobby to really showcase the old boy."

"If you say so," Ben said. "Looks like he might give the kids nightmares or something."

Ms. Merritt shot the man a look that said he was out of line.

"Sorry, I just think … Well, don't you think he looks a little vicious for a middle school mascot?"

"Moving on…" Ms. Merritt pressed forward with the conversation, ignoring Ben's question. "The trophies will need to be boxed up. I'll have to weed through them over summer break to see which ones will fit in the new trophy case."

From her crouched position behind the stack of wood, Nova's stomach began to roil and rumble loudly. She felt like she was past the puking stage, but desperately needed water and was helpless to quiet her stomach's angry growls. Fear gripped her. What if they could hear her stomach? What would she say to explain why she was down here?

"What about this memorial?" Ben asked, pointing to something behind the glass.

Ms. Merritt moved to stand next to the man.

"That can go in the garbage," she replied.

"The garbage? That doesn't seem right. That poor girl died, right here in this school. I was thinking you might want us to make a special spot to display her picture. I mean, it's really sad."

"I understand what you are saying, Ben!" Ms. Merritt snapped. "I attended school with the girl. We were in the same grade. And yes, while very sad indeed, no one remembers Evelyn Chambers. Her parents are deceased. She certainly means nothing to future Panthers. Get rid of it."

"If you say—" Ben started, but Ms. Merritt cut him off.

"Are we done here, Ben? I've got a budget meeting in less than five minutes."

"Yes, ma'am. That's all I needed. We'll get started on this wing tomorrow morning," Ben said, hurrying after Ms. Merritt, who started walking away before he finished his sentence.

The echo of Ms. Merritt's high-heeled footfalls faded as the two departed. Nova rose and moved cautiously toward the trophy case. The first thing that grabbed her attention was the life-size panther. The sculpture was so realistic, with its bared teeth and sleek black fur. The animal looked like he was on the prowl, his back legs on one shelf, one front leg on the shelf below, while the other clawed paw sat poised and ready to strike. Nova had to agree with Ben. The beast gave off more of a nightmare vibe than a friendly mascot.

There were trophies dating back to long before Nova was even born. Sculpted, bronze footballs, basketball hoops, and soccer balls sat atop bases proclaiming the winning championships. Tucked among the trophies was a plaque. It read:

Evelyn Chambers
Forever in our hearts, forever a Panther
1973-1985
In loving memory

Tears welled up in Nova's eyes. A girl her age had lost her life, right here in this school according to Ben. It was so sad. Her eyes scanned the words again until she reached the photo sitting atop the sentiment. A chill raced up her back and goosebumps rose on her arms. The girl in the picture, Evelyn Chambers, the poor soul who died all those years ago here in the halls of this school, was the same girl she saw at Ayden's house and on the school bus—the same girl who confronted Nova in the abandoned restroom minutes ago.

Nova backed away from the trophy case, almost tripping over a sledgehammer lying on the ground. Sour bile rose in her throat, but she swallowed it down, turned, and ran as fast as she could in her weakened state. She didn't stop until she reached the nurse's office where she collapsed on the cot.

Chapter 10

On the ride home, Nova stretched out across the back seat of her mom's car and covered her head with her coat. She was surprised her mom wasn't too put out about missing most of her shift. But as usual, her mom fretted about how Nova had consumed gluten.

"I don't understand," her mom started as soon as they pulled out of the school parking lot. "We're so careful, right? You're careful, aren't you? I know I'm careful." She didn't wait for Nova's response.

"I mean, I guess I haven't checked the labels of many of your go-to's in a while. Maybe something we've counted on to be GF changed their recipe. It happens, you know. I'll never understand why—"

Nova pulled the coat off her face. "No, Mom, it wasn't your fault. I guess if anything, it was my fault."

"Your fault? Did you knowingly eat something you knew would make you sick? The doctors warned me about that. I never believed them when they said the teen years were tough on kids with celiac, that you might eat normal food due to peer pressure or … I don't know. Silly me, I always thought, 'Not my kid, she'd never—'"

"Mom!" Nova tried to get a word in.

"But, well, here we are. I'm sorry, sweetie. I know it's tempting."

"Mom! Please!"

Mom fell silent.

"Someone at school gave me cookies she said were gluten-free."

"What? You never eat food you are uncertain about. Why would you trust it? Cross-contamination … hidden ingredients … lack of knowledge—"

"I know, Mom. They were in a package labeled gluten-free. I'd had them before, but this time…"

"I don't understand, Nova," Mom said thoughtfully.

"Yeah, I think she put regular cookies in the package. I fell for it. It's my fault."

Nova saw the shock on her mother's face in the rearview mirror. She was quiet for a bit, processing what Nova told her as she parked the car in her spot at the apartment complex.

"You mean, she did it on purpose?" Mom asked. The question came out slowly, with a pause of disbelief between each word. Nova saw her mother's brow furrow as she shook her head. Nova could tell she was unable to comprehend how someone would knowingly make her daughter sick. She took the key out of the ignition and turned to look at Nova.

"It's a long story, Mom. I need to rest. I'll tell you all about it when I'm feeling better, okay?"

"Sure, I'm sorry. Let's get you in some comfortable clothes and into bed."

Nova was relieved her mom was willing to drop the conversation for now. In truth, Nova herself was having a hard time believing someone would do this to her on purpose, even though she knew it was Caitlyn's fear of losing the solo that prompted her to do something so mean.

She went straight to her bedroom, kicking off her shoes and removing her school clothes as she made her way to her dresser. Then she grabbed her most comfortable hoodie and sweatpants, pulling them on with weakened limbs before falling into bed. Mom followed closely behind her, gathering up the clothing and turning the bedside lamp on.

"I'll be right back," her mom said as she dumped Nova's clothes in the hamper.

Nova wiggled under the covers; extreme fatigue made her limbs feel heavy. She felt like she was moving in slow motion. Before she knew it, her mom came back with a tray of all the things they used to comfort Nova after a gluten episode.

"Peppermint tea, Children's Pepto, a hot water bottle, and some water," her mom said as she unloaded each item from the tray, placing them on the nightstand. She set the tray down and fluffed Nova's pillow, before putting the hot water bottle on Nova's stomach and pulling the blankets up around her chin. "Can you think of anything else you need?"

It took every ounce of strength Nova had left to mumble, "No, Mom, I'm good. Just need to rest." Her eyes felt heavy, and she was half asleep as she whispered, "Thank you."

Her mom leaned in and kissed Nova on her forehead. "I'm so sorry you feel so badly. Sleep it off, sweet girl."

Mom tiptoed out of the room, quietly shutting the door behind her. Nova fell into a deep sleep.

When she woke, it was dark outside. She grabbed her

phone and silently scolded herself for not connecting the charger before she passed out. There wasn't much battery life left, but the phone told her it was four-thirty in the morning. She'd been asleep for over twelve hours. In addition to missing a FaceTime request from Ceci, she missed five calls from Ayden, but he'd sent her several texts. She grabbed a water bottle and chugged it as she read his messages.

> AYDEN: Heard you tossed your cookies at school today, literally.

She choked on her drink as she laughed at his first text, then grimaced and grabbed her stomach. Her muscles were sore like she'd done hundreds of sit-ups.

> AYDEN: Too soon? Yeah, probably. My bad.

This time, she spit the liquid out, and it dribbled down her chin as she was unable to contain her laughter.

> AYDEN: So, good news, bad news.

She muttered to the empty room, "Bad news first."

> AYDEN: Guessing you want the bad news first.

She chuckled again—how well he knew her.

> AYDEN: Bad news ... Mrs. Hastings had to leave before auditions. Her kid had a fever or something.

Nova frowned, feeling sorry for her teacher and her son.

AYDEN: Good news … She had to postpone auditions for the spring concert.

Her heart rate quickened, and a smile broke on her pale face. She'd have the chance to audition after all. Caitlyn's evil scheme had failed. She couldn't help but feel satisfaction, despite feeling bad for Mrs. Hastings.

AYDEN: So purge those gluten demons quickly! Second chance day after tomorrow. You're going to kill it. Feel better!

Nova grabbed another water bottle and gulped it down in record time. Feeling satisfied this experience wouldn't ruin her chances of landing a solo, she fell back on her pillow and was soon fast asleep.

The morning sun cut a divide across her bedroom, a bright beam settling on her face and waking her. As anticipated, her head throbbed to its own dull beat. She greedily drank another bottle of water and was reaching for the next when her mother knocked gently on her door before poking her head in. She was dressed for work in pale pink scrubs; her brown hair, which had been invaded by wavy strands of white in just a few months, was pulled back in a tight bun.

"Good morning?" she said. "At least I hope it's a good morning. How are you feeling?"

"Worse than most, actually," she replied, pushing the blankets off and sitting on the edge of the bed for a moment to make sure she wasn't too dizzy to stand.

"Well, I've already called the school to let them know you wouldn't be in today."

"Thanks, Mom."

"I really can't miss another day, and I don't want you to be alone all day. So I'm declaring a take your daughter to work day!" Her mother spoke in her cheery voice as if that would make all the difference in the world to Nova.

"Ugh!" Nova moaned, throwing herself back into her bed. "Seriously, I think I'll be fine here by myself."

"Well, that makes one of us. Come on, it won't be that bad. You can be the bingo caller this afternoon. Nan's friends will love it!"

"That's a stretch. How about I hide out in Nan's room all day with a book?"

"Suit yourself," Mom said. "Get up and get ready. I'll go put some bread in your toaster while you get dressed. I'm sure you're starving,"

Nova's stomach rumbled its reply loudly as Mom disappeared, closing the door behind her. Nova dressed in leggings and an oversized hoodie and went to the kitchen. Two pieces of perfectly toasted bread popped up from her toaster. Her mom used bright pink nail polish to paint the words, 'NO GLUTEN!' on the outside of the appliance. Mom made all their meals gluten-free since Nova's diagnosis. She was barely two years old when doctors uncovered the reason why she failed to gain weight and struggled with constant stomach pain. Mom tried to eat only gluten-free items herself but had been unable to give up regular bread. The tiny kitchen held two toasters for that reason. Even crumbs shared by a toaster would trigger Nova's immune system to rebel.

She smeared a spoonful of peanut butter on the gluten-free toast and took another water bottle from the fridge before grabbing her bag and meeting her mother at the front door. She didn't feel horrible, just weak, and she always needed a day of recovery after accidentally ingesting gluten. She couldn't be in a classroom. For the next several hours, she knew her brain wouldn't be firing synapses properly. Her mom called it brain fog. Nova called herself lame-brained. She couldn't focus—thoughts flitted away and trying to concentrate on lectures or directions was pointless.

She didn't know why she even bothered to bring her schoolwork and a book. A day spent watching ridiculous game shows with Nan was all her fuzzy brain would be able to accomplish today.

Chapter 11

At the nursing home, Mom made the rounds to all her coworkers, introducing Nova and explaining that while her daughter wasn't contagious sick, she couldn't go to school.

"I promise it's nothing catching," she pleaded with everyone. "She got glutened yesterday and needs to rest."

While the head nurse side-eyed a bit more than anyone else, she didn't question the girl's presence any further.

Nova walked the brightly lit hall, trying to avert her eyes from the opened doors that lined the corridor. It always felt like spying. She wondered why the residents kept their doors open. Some were bedridden, while others sat in chairs staring out their window or at their television. Nova thought maybe they were so lonely that even the glimpse of someone different kept them bound to the world outside these walls.

While the rooms were arranged and decorated differently, the entire center had the same smell. The antiseptic aroma reminded Nova of hospitals. Hiding below that familiar scent lingered something more uncertain. A heavy mix of countless perfumes and after-shaves mingled with something far less pleasant. A smell so organic and final, everyone seemed to have grown nose-blind to it. The smell permeated Nova's senses though, and she tried her best not to think of what the odor might be.

Nan's door was also open. Nova knocked on the door's trim. She never knew who she would be met by when visiting Nan. Some days, Nan herself seemed bogged down by a brain fog so intense there was no getting through to her. Other times, she appeared to recognize Nova but spoke only of times Nova barely remembered, as she'd been so young. And still other days, she was the sharp, feisty woman she used to be. Today started well.

"Who's there?" Nan called out in a sweet voice.

"It's me, Nova," she replied, entering the sun-filled room.

"Oh, Nova!" Nan said, slowly rising from her recliner.

"No need to get up, Nan."

"Nonsense. I need a hug from my favorite grand-daughter!"

"I'm your only granddaughter, Nan," Nova said with a laugh.

"That may well be, but you're still my favorite."

Nova was surprised to see she was now taller than her grandmother and wondered how that had happened so quickly. She wrapped the tiny woman gently in her arms. Nan felt so fragile, as if Nova could bruise her mottled skin with an embrace.

"What did I do to deserve a visit from my favorite granddaughter? Is it a holiday? My birthday?"

Nova's body tensed. How could she explain to her grandma it wasn't a special occasion? And would she understand? Nan reached up and put her cold hands on Nova's face.

"Relax, I'm just messing with you," she said. A spark of youth glimmered in her eyes.

"Oh, right, good one, Nan. I had to stay home from school today. I accidentally ate some gluten yesterday."

"Well, that's a shame. I've heard people with celiac disease should avoid gluten," Nan said while she shuffled back to her recliner. As she slowly lowered herself into the seat, she looked up at Nova with the same girlish expression. "Gotcha again."

Nova couldn't control the grin that spread across her face. She was happy to see Nan was having a 'good day.' Mom had warned her the good days were getting fewer and farther between.

"You make yourself comfortable there on the couch. My show is about to start. It'll be nice to have someone here to play along with me."

With shaky hands, Nan pointed the remote control at her small television. Although the volume was set at an ear-splitting level when the TV came on, Nan punched the volume-up button several times.

"That man simply doesn't age," Nan commented about the game show's host.

Nova fluffed the pillows on the old, familiar couch. She was certain Nan held a little tighter to the loosening threads in her mind since she was able to fill her room with her own furniture and what she called 'do-dads.' Nan did her best to arrange the room just as it appeared in her home before she conceded to moving to the nursing home.

There was a quiet knock on the door. It was Mom, and she didn't wait for an answer. She walked past Nova, shaking her head, and went to where Nan sat enthralled in her program.

"Mom, what have I told you about the volume? I can hear this four doors down. It isn't good for your ears."

Mom went to the television and quickly lowered the volume, shaking Nan from her game show-induced trance.

"Oh look, it's my favorite daughter!"

"Good morning, Nan. You seem well today."

"I feel well as well," Nan commented. Her eyes finally moved from the television with the start of a commercial.

"Nova is going to keep you company today. I hope you don't mind."

"Don't mind at all. Heard you tried to poison her last night."

Nova and her mother struck matching shocked expressions.

"I swear, I didn't tell her a thing!" Nova laughed.

"It wasn't me who tried to poison her. She tells me it was a classmate. I've requested an appointment with the school principal to discuss the matter further."

"Mom," Nova said with a dramatic eye roll. She wanted to forget about the whole thing. Especially the part that came when she was alone in the bathroom. She'd been too sick to let her mind wander back to the girl who seemed to pop up everywhere she went. Now knowing the girl was dead frightened her more than ever.

"Now, Nova, the school needs to know to be more careful. And I think the girl who pulled the switcheroo with the cookies needs to be held accountable. I asked to speak to the school nurse as well, but apparently, she's on medical leave."

Nova knew it wasn't worth the battle. Once her mom's mind was made up, there was no talking her down.

"Just promise me you won't use the word switcheroo, please."

"You two stay out of trouble today," Mom pressed on, ignoring Nova's plea. "I brought you both some ginger ale, and I'll come in on my lunch break and see how things are going."

"Thanks, Mom," Nova said as her mom left the room. Nan didn't reply; she was busy searching for the volume button on the remote.

Nova and Nan passed the next hour competing against each other and the guests on two game shows. Before a new show started, a young woman entered the room.

"Nan, I've got your morning medicines," the woman said in a sing-song voice.

"Hope you brought me something better than an iron pill and heartburn meds," Nan protested.

"Don't go sassing me, young lady," the nurse replied, casting a wink at Nova.

Nova saw the woman's name tag read, *Tasha*.

"Is this your twin sister visiting you today?" Tasha asked as she waited for Nan to take the small cup from her. The nurse held Nan's water cup up, and Nova's grandmother made an exaggerated effort to swallow the pills.

"Don't be daft, woman. She's my older sister," Nan joked.

"Of course, of course, now I see it," Tasha replied. "She's almost as beautiful as you."

"I'm Nova, Nan's granddaughter," Nova chimed in.

"Oh, yes! Your mom works here! I see the resemblance now."

"Just feeling a little off today, so I'm hanging out with Nan."

"Well, I'm sorry to hear you are under the weather, but you couldn't spend the day with a more wonderful woman. I'm kind of new to town too, and your grandmother knows every bit of gossip about every single person who lives here. She should've written a book. She's a regular town historian."

"Oh, stop it now, Tasha," Nan interjected. "Your time would be better spent buttering up Mr. Pasqual across the hall."

"Well, alright. You don't need anything else today? Any laundry I can take for you?"

"Nothing I can think of at the moment, Tasha," Nan said. "Thank you, dear."

"You're very welcome. It was nice meeting you, Nova. I hope you feel better soon."

Tasha left the room. Nova took the opportunity to pick Nan's brain when another commercial interrupted her game show.

"Is that true what Tasha said, Nan? You know a lot about this town and its history?"

"Well, I've lived here all my life and I must have a face that says, 'tell me everything,' because I know the secrets of many, I suppose."

A news break broke into the program and Nan pushed the mute button on the remote, allowing Nova a minute to figure out what to say next.

Nova went with the direct approach. "Do you know anything about a girl who died at my school?" Nan was quiet for some time before speaking.

"Yes … Yes, there was a young girl who passed away at the school. That was a long time ago. How did you hear about it?"

"Oh, uh, I saw the memorial in the trophy case," Nova said, responding quickly, surprised that her lame-brain allowed her to think on her feet. She probably could tell Nan she believed the ghost of Evelyn Chambers was haunting her but didn't want to muddy the story and also didn't want her mom to find out.

"I see. It was a tragic thing. The poor girl was allergic

to peanuts. Somehow she was exposed to peanuts one day and died of anaphylaxis before anyone could help her. She'd have been about your age when she died. The whole town was shaken up over it. So senseless and scary."

Nova sensed Nan was inside herself as if she had been transported back to the time when poor Evelyn Chambers didn't make it home from school one day.

"Wow, that is sad. Did they ever figure out what happened? How she ate something with peanuts in it?" Nova asked.

"Not that I recall, no. It was chalked up to an accident. The nurse didn't get to her in time. She was the first student to have an EpiPen at school; those things were a brand-new medical miracle at that time. Such a small detail that could've saved her life. By the time the nurse got it to her, it was too late."

A sunbeam through the window brushed Nan's cheek, catching the single tear that slid down her face, making it glisten. Nan didn't wipe it away. Her grandmother's words played over in Nova's mind. She was so lost in thought; she didn't take notice of the silence. From her chair by the window, Nan gave a soft snuffle, bringing Nova back to the moment. Nan nodded off. Nova went to her and tucked the crocheted blanket around her shoulders before making her way to the couch.

She pulled out her phone and searched for any information about Evelyn Chambers and her sad fate. There was little online, except for a short newspaper article that outlined the facts. Nan had gotten them all spot on, so there wasn't much to take away except the picture of Evelyn Chambers. She recognized the girl immediately. Her mind wrangled with the revelations, and she came to realize she couldn't be hallucinating Evelyn's presence.

She'd never seen a picture of the girl until she saw the etched face on the memorial plaque. Maybe it was her gluten lame-brain that kept her from putting two-and-two together at the time. If Evelyn was a figment of her imagination, there was no chance Nova could have conjured up an aberration in the exact image of the real Evelyn. She was now certain Evelyn Chambers had been following her for weeks.

She now knew who was haunting her but wasn't sure how she would ever figure out how to help her. And while it was scary to think a dead girl was reaching out to her, she knew Evelyn Chambers didn't mean her any harm. She'd only ever seemed sad when Nova saw her, not angry or vengeful, at least not toward Nova.

Nan slept until Mom showed up with a lunch tray and a paper bag full of gluten-free snacks.

"I couldn't find much in the cafeteria that was gluten-free except for an apple. Good thing I keep a stash of GF goodies in my car. My mom card is going to get pulled for allowing my child to eat nothing but chips and candy bars for lunch."

"I think the apple will save you," Nova replied.

"Nan," Mom spoke softly to her mother. "Are you ready for some lunch?"

Nan startled and was confused upon waking.

"What's that, dear?" she asked.

"I brought your lunch," Mom replied, setting the tray on the side table before positioning the TV tray in front of her mom.

"Smells good, Nan," Nova said as Mom lifted the dome cover from the tray.

Nan adjusted her glasses and peered at Nova. Her expression spoke for her—confusion and fear.

Nova went to her grandmother and took her hand.

"Nan, it's me, Nova."

"Oh, yes." A tiny spark of recognition flashed in her eyes. "Nova, you should come to see me more often, child. You look like you've grown a foot taller since I saw you last."

Mom, who was busying herself opening a packet of salad dressing, looked up at Nova. So much emotion swept over her mother's face, and she mouthed the word *sorry*.

After Nan ate her lunch, Nova practiced the piece she chose for the audition. Nan enjoyed the song. She tapped her foot in rhythm and closed her eyes; her smile was true. Nova thought she might be helping soothe her grandmother's mind. When the third rendition of the song was complete, a smattering of applause arose behind her.

Nova turned to see a small crowd gathered outside Nan's door. One elderly gentleman put his fingers in his mouth and let out a robust whistle, while a woman in a wheelchair exclaimed, "Bravo! Encore!"

Rather than be embarrassed by the attention, Nova curtsied to the group and sang the song again, this time with more energy and feeling. She was grateful to have an audience and happy she brought some joy into the residents' day. As she finished singing, Mom showed up, gently easing her way through the group that appeared to have grown since she began singing.

"That's my girl," she whispered to every one of the elderly residents who gathered to hear Nova sing.

Nova bowed to the group again and nodded to each of them in thanks.

Despite the obvious enjoyment Nan showed as Nova sang, the Nan who woke up from a brief nap was not the same Nan who greeted her earlier that morning. As the day passed, the true Nan grew further and further away. While it broke Nova's heart to see her that way, she clung to the memory of the playful banter they shared hours ago, committing her wisecracks and laughter to memory while being grateful Nan was lucid enough to provide Nova with the biggest clue she had about the life and death of Evelyn Chambers.

Chapter 12

A cluster of kids huddled around the door to the music classroom, each clamoring to see the cast list posted outside Mrs. Hastings's door. Some walked away with smiles and pats on the back, while a few withdrew with slumped shoulders and few words. Caitlyn and her concert choir clique parted, leaving a clear path for Nova and Ayden to approach the paper pinned to the wall. Caitlyn's eyes bore into Nova with a burning scowl.

"Well, this is an interesting turn of events," Ayden said, tapping the top line of the list. "There's never been a duet in the spring concert, at least not to my appallingly uninformed knowledge, that is."

"A duet?" Nova asked, scanning the document. There it was. She did not get the solo she hoped for, but neither did Caitlyn. The two would be singing a song together in the production. Now Nova understood why Caitlyn was staring her down.

Caitlyn approached, her arms folded tightly over her chest, cheeks flushed a vibrant red. The group that usually followed her closely fell back, as if sensing a confrontation brewing.

"Congratulations, Nova," Caitlyn sneered. "I'm not sure what led Mrs. Hastings to make this unfortunate decision, but it looks as if we will be working closely together soon."

Nova stood frozen, grasping for words. She was pleased she'd have the opportunity to stand out in the production, but not at all thrilled she would be sharing a microphone with the mean girl.

"Caitlyn," Ayden interjected, helping his speechless friend out. "Your seething envy is showing. You might want to go splash some cold water on your face before you spontaneously combust."

Now it was Caitlyn who was lost for words. She let out a forceful humph before turning and stomping off. As she made her way across the hall, she lurched forward as if someone shoved her hard. She almost lost her footing but regained her balance before falling to the floor. Her head snapped around to blast the person who shoved her, but shock spread across her face. There was no one standing close enough to push her. She snorted again, straightened herself, and caught up to her friends.

"That was weird," Ayden said. "It's like she tripped on her own ego or something."

Nova remembered the first day on the bus when Caitlyn's ponytail was yanked by an unseen hand. As she turned to head back up the hallway for her next class, something in the narrow window to Mrs. Hastings's classroom caught her eye. It was Evelyn Chambers, watching from the window with a satisfied smirk on her face. The girl's expression gave Nova the chills.

Just then, an announcement came over the loudspeaker.

"Nova Eckley, please report to the principal's office. Nova Eckley, to the principal's office."

"Ooh, what'd you do?" Ayden questioned, his eyes wide.

"No clue."

She moved through the crowded breezeway, feeling every set of curious eyes that fell on her as she passed. Through the glass doors that led into the office foyer, she saw her mom sitting outside Principal Merritt's door. She groaned, not wanting to face the confrontation her mother insisted was necessary.

"Mom," she whispered, taking a seat next to her mother. "I told you I didn't want to make a big deal out of this. I'm fine now—"

"I'm glad you are fine now. I love that you were able to make it to the audition yesterday, but you had to miss a day and a half of school. Not to mention the pain you were in. It's unacceptable, and that girl needs to be punished for her actions."

According to Caitlyn, she already is being punished for her actions, Nova thought. But before she could open her mouth to tell her mom what had transpired this morning, the door to the principal's office opened and Ms. Merritt appeared with a wide smile that seemed almost predatory to Nova. The woman exuded all the warmth of the creepy Panther mascot.

"Mrs. Eckley, Nova, come right in. It's so good to see you both."

Nova didn't believe that last part. She was certain Ms. Merritt would rather avoid this conversation completely.

"Have a seat," Ms. Merritt instructed. "I do apologize for Nurse Brumley. She's dealing with some, well, I guess you'd say health issues of her own. We aren't sure when she'll be back, to be honest. For now, my secretary is doing her best to keep up with her own job and that of Nurse Brumley. It isn't ideal, to say the least."

Nova and her mom sat next to each other. Nova couldn't force herself to make eye contact with Ms. Merritt. She hated confrontation and had a feeling this conversation might not go as Mom planned.

"I understand you were under the weather earlier this week, Nova. I'm so sorry to hear that, but you seem to be fine today, which is wonderful."

Nova couldn't think of a reply. Fortunately for her, she didn't have to speak. Mom butted in, speaking over Ms. Merritt's comments.

"With all due respect, Ms. Merritt, she wasn't simply under the weather. She has an autoimmune disease. Her symptoms are almost nonexistent—until, that is, she consumes anything containing gluten."

"An autoimmune disease? It was my understanding it was an allergy," Ms. Merritt said, shuffling through a file folder. "I'm looking for a 504 Plan. I assume you know what that is. I don't see the paperwork in her file, however."

"No, it is similar to an allergy, but her body reacts very badly. As with most autoimmune diseases, the body turns on itself. With her, it's when gluten is introduced. It is extremely painful and can be dangerous. And yes, I know what a 504 Plan is. We do not have one, as her well-being was never a problem at her old school. Everyone there bent over backward to keep Nova safe."

Her mother was working herself up. The passion for protecting her child rang clear through her shaky voice. Nova reached over and took her mother's hand in hopes of calming her down.

"I see. Well, that does sound horrible. I'm so very sorry, but I fail to see why this is a school matter. Did she eat food from the cafeteria? If she made a poor decision concerning her health, well, that sounds like something that needs to be addressed with Nova and perhaps her doctor, Mrs. Eckley. Without a 504, there is little more we can do."

Nova saw red rising on her mother's cheeks. She squeezed the arms of her chair in a death grip. Mom was about to blow.

"No, Ms. Merritt," Nova finally spoke, giving her mother a moment to collect herself. "I didn't eat something from the school—"

"Well then, I am not sure what you want me to do about this."

"She was tricked!" Mom's voice rose as she tried to make Ms. Merritt understand. "Tricked by a fellow student!"

"Is this true, Nova? And if so, how exactly were you tricked?"

"Well, someone brought a package of cookies that were labeled gluten-free, but she replaced the gluten-free cookies with ones that contained gluten."

"That's a serious allegation, Nova," Ms. Merritt said.

"Yes, well, it's a serious issue for Nova! And for another student to do so intentionally, well, I can't wrap my mind around it, to be honest," Mom said. Nova saw her mother was fighting to stay composed.

"Intentionally?" Ms. Merritt said, leaning back in her chair. "I can't see any of our students doing such a thing intentionally. Who gave you the cookies, Nova?"

Nova shrunk in her seat, wishing the ground would open and swallow her whole.

"I don't think I should point fingers," Nova said.

"Point fingers? Nova, you know who gave you the cookies," her mom said. "It isn't considered finger-pointing if the person actually did something wrong, which she obviously did."

"Yeah, but—"

"Your mother is right, Nova. There is no way to get to the bottom of this unless we have the complete story," Ms. Merritt interjected.

Nova's face flushed with anxiety. She should have tried harder to convince her mother not to report the cookie debacle. If Caitlyn was punished for what she did, Nova couldn't imagine what the girl's retaliation might be. Still, the thing that stressed Nova out the most was the realization that for whatever reason, she was being haunted. By that comparison, Caitlyn wasn't scary at all.

The room went silent. The pressure weighed heavy on Nova, and she wished she could jump up and run. But she knew there was only one way to escape this nightmare, so she spoke.

"Caitlyn," she whispered, her eyes cast down to her lap. She tried to soothe herself and release the tension by busily rubbing her hands together.

"I'm sorry. Did you say Caitlyn, as in Caitlyn Rogers?" Ms. Merritt said. Disbelief rang in her tone, and she pressed her palms onto her desktop.

Nova nodded her head, her eyes still focused on her hands. The heat of Ms. Merritt's glare bore into her, and a bead of sweat slipped down the back of her neck.

"Well, now, I don't know what to think about that."

"Who is Caitlyn Rogers?" Mom asked.

Ms. Merritt pressed on in her defense of Caitlyn, ignoring the question. She rose from her seat and moved to the front of the desk where she leaned casually against it and crossed her legs, clasping her hands together.

"I am certain the whole thing was a misunderstanding.

Ms. Rogers would never do such a thing on purpose. She's one of our best students."

The words left Ms. Merritt's mouth on a wave of scornful indignation. Nova felt the woman's breath as she spoke, and felt small in the woman's shadow.

"Are you accusing my daughter of lying?" she asked.

Nova shifted her eyes, glancing at her mom sensing the anger in her voice, willing her to stay calm.

"Certainly not, Mrs. Eckley," Ms. Merritt said, attempting to placate the woman. "I'm sure it was an honest mistake. Caitlyn has never been in trouble at school."

"Well, something happened that caused my daughter to become horribly sick and miss a day and a half of her education. I find it hard to believe that swapping out the cookies was an honest mistake."

I see your point, but it's impossible to prove." Ms. Merritt pushed off the desk, turning her back to Nova and her mom. She walked to the window, separating the blinds and peering outside for a moment before turning back to Nova and her mom. "I mean, I still can't believe it was Caitlyn to begin with, and I can't punish a child, a child with an impeccable school record, I might add, for doing something when the intent cannot be deemed malicious."

"So that's it? You aren't going to do anything to get to the bottom of it all?"

"I'm not exactly sure what I can do, but I will have a conversation with Caitlyn." Ms. Merritt seemed to believe the meeting was over. She returned to the window and again used her fingers to separate the blinds, peeking out. Nova believed the principal was excusing them in action if not in direct words.

Nova happened a glance up and choked back a gasp. Evelyn Chamber's wispy presence stared back at Ms.

Merritt; her face angry and fiery. Nova was certain Ms. Merritt had to see the ghostly apparition. Ice crystals formed on the window blocking the principal's view. The woman lifted a finger and scratched at the frost with a perfectly manicured, bright red fingernail before turning back and pulling her cardigan around her. The look on her face told Nova that she hadn't seen the figure of the girl, but she was surprised to see Nova and her mom still sitting in her office.

Nova's mom didn't acknowledge the dismissal as Nova had.

"Well, I hope that conversation can include how her 'honest mistake' caused poor Nova hours of horrible pain. She needs to understand how dangerous food bullying can…"

"Food bullying?" Ms. Merritt cut Mom off. She returned to her seat. "That's a bit of an overstatement."

"Call it what you like. I want the point stressed to the girl that her actions were dangerous and cruel."

"I said I will speak to her, Mrs. Eckley. I don't think there is anything more I can do."

Mom stood up, snatched her purse off the floor and made her way to the door. Nova wasn't sure if she should get up and follow or stay where she was, but quickly decided she wanted nothing more than to be out of the office, so she followed her mother and kept her head down. Mom opened the door, then turned back to the principal. Nova could see there was something more her mother wanted to say, but she was angry and frustrated and couldn't come up with the perfect parting words to drive her point home.

"I assure you, Mrs. Eckley, the safety of my students and staff is of utmost importance to me," she said, rising from her chair.

Nova saw a snarky grin flash on the principal's face.

"I'm glad you are feeling better, Nova. And congratulations on your duet."

Nova struggled to keep up with her mother's pace as she followed her out of the office. Once in the hall, Nova closed the gap between them.

"Mom, I'm really sorry that went down like that. I should have kept quiet."

"No, Nova, you did the right thing by telling me. Something about that woman is just, I don't know, off."

"I need to stand up for myself more. I let my guard down when I should have been more cautious."

"Oh, honey, stop blaming yourself."

Nova and her mom jumped when the bell let out its ear-splitting ring. The empty hallway was quickly brought to life by dozens of noisy students pouring out the classroom doors.

"I've got to get to work. Have a good day, and don't eat anything you didn't bring from home."

Nova wanted to hug her mom, but there were too many eyes checking out an unfamiliar adult in the hallway. A group of kids crowded between Nova and her mother. Nova drew an imaginary cross across her chest and mouthed the words, *cross my heart,* before the two turned and went their separate ways.

Nova went about her day intent on avoiding any run-ins with Caitlyn. In the cafeteria, she went the long way around to get to the table where Ayden sat so she didn't have to pass too closely to the choir table.

"You feeling better now?" Ayden asked as she sat across from him.

"Physically, yes."

"I thought you'd be hyped today. I mean, I know you

wanted a solo, but a duet is the next best thing. Oh, except it's with Caitlyn—"

"Yeah, I'm excited about that, but the Caitlyn part isn't ideal and isn't going to improve after what happened this morning." Nova fiddled with the zipper of her lunch bag but didn't open it. Typically, she was ravenous after an episode of being glutened, but she wasn't hungry. It was as if her whole body was full of nervous energy. Not the good kind, the kind that came from dread.

"Do tell," Ayden said, setting his sandwich down. His eyes widened as he leaned across the table.

"My mother had a meeting with Principal Merritt earlier today."

"About Caitlyn? Have to say, I'm siding with Moms on this one. Caitlyn needs to be put in her place. What she did was beyond uncool."

"I know. I want to forget it ever happened, though. The last thing I need is more bad blood between us."

"I get it. So what happened?"

While she wasn't ready to eat anything, her mouth was suddenly dry and she broke into her tote, removing a water bottle and gulping it down before she continued. Ayden's expression didn't change. He sat, mouth open and eyes wide, eager for her to tell him more.

"Nothing really. Ms. Merritt sounded like she didn't even believe the golden child could have done something. Total denial."

"Sounds about right," Ayden said, picking his sandwich up and inspecting it before he took a bite. "I could talk to my mom about it if you want," he said with his mouth full.

"No, no one else needs talking to. I thought my mom was going to stroke out right there."

"So, that's it? Instead of getting detention, she's going to be named Student of the Month again?"

"I don't know. She told my mom she would have a talk with Caitlyn, but who knows?"

Nova got lost in thought wondering how she could tell Ayden the most terrifying part of her experience with Caitlyn's cookie prank. Ever since her talk with Nan, she'd felt on edge. Jumping at loud sounds, gasping at shadows. She needed to talk to someone about the strange events and how she thought she was being recruited to help a ghost, for lack of a better word. Ayden was the only person she could tell, but she was scared. What if he thought she was hallucinating or didn't believe her, or worse?

She barely touched her lunch, and the two didn't say anything else for the remainder of the period. Nova glanced at the clock and saw the bell would ring in two minutes. Despite this knowledge, it took her by surprise again, and the two of them jumped when it rang.

They both burst into laughter.

"That bell has got to go," Ayden said.

"Agreed! See you in choir."

Caitlyn wasn't in choir that afternoon. Nova overheard Ainsley and Layla saying Caitlyn had an orthodontist appointment. The two girls groaned about how lucky Caitlyn was to be getting clear aligners. Their complaints about their metal braces were cut off by Mrs. Hastings. Nova felt some of the tension escape her; Caitlyn wouldn't be on the bus today. She hoped to avoid her nemesis for as long as possible, knowing her lucky streak couldn't last much longer. But she was relieved to make it through the day without a run-in.

Chapter 13

That evening, Nova finished the makeup work from her absence. Despite missing a day and a half, it didn't take her long to complete the assignments. She reheated some leftovers Mom saved for her. As she finished rinsing her dishes and putting them in the dishwasher, she got a FaceTime notification. It was Ceci! Nova hurriedly answered the call, eager to catch up with her friend.

"Hey, Ceci," she said cheerfully, "how's it going?"

"How's it going? How about where have you been? I tried to call you the other night. You ghosting me? Me, your best friend in the whole wide world? I'm crushed."

Nova knew her friend was being sarcastic, but for fun, she played along.

"Yeah, well, I'm so busy making new best friends, like ones who are way cooler than you, trying to decide who to go out with every weekend and just, you know, moving on. It's time, right? To move on—"

"Oh, right," Ceci said, nodding her head. "So that whole blood oath promise we made when we were seven is canceled now, huh? Because I thought it was binding. I mean, you still have a scar on the palm of your hand and all."

"Yes, I do have a scar on my hand still," she replied, holding her hand up and squinting at her palm, searching for the scar that hadn't entirely faded. "If I remember correctly, you don't have the matching scar. Why was that again? Oh, right, you flaked out. See, there's a reason why they say blood is thicker than water. The fact that you were a wimp and didn't make the cut, choosing instead to spit on your palm and shake on it … Well, in my opinion, it's not the same."

Neither girl could keep a straight face any longer and laughed off their conversation.

"Okay, so the real story is I got glutened," Nova said, "I spent hours in the bathroom—"

"Spare me the gory details," Ceci said, scrunching her nose and flapping her hand. "I know all about the aftermath … being your BFF and all."

"Well, this time the barf-fest wasn't the scariest part."

"Really? Spill."

Nova rehashed how she found the forgotten bathroom and was joined by the ghostly girl. Ceci sat in rapt attention, hands on her chin, her mouth forming a perfect 'O' and her eyes bugging at all the proper moments.

"Okay, I don't know how you are keeping it together. If I had some ghostly specter following me around the school —into the bathroom, no less—I'd be done. Just done, like home school here I come. Uh-uh, no way."

"Yeah, it's beyond creepy. I guess I'm dealing because I don't think she means me harm. I mean, she'd never hurt me. She's made me jump out of my skin more times than I can count, though. Come to think of it, the insanely loud school bell has actually given me more jump scares than the ghost."

"You need to have your apartment blessed!"

"Well, that's the other part that keeps me from flipping out. I've never seen her at my apartment. I've seen her at school, and I can feel her sitting next to me on the bus. One time I even saw her at Ayden's house, which doesn't make a whole lot of sense. And then I saw her outside the principal's office. Yeah, she's pretty pushy."

"Okay, well, guess no one would be too hyped about having the entire school blessed. And a bus? I don't even think that's a thing. I don't know, I'm no ghost hunter, but I've watched plenty of scary movies and usually the preacher man sprinkles holy water and stuff."

"Well, here's where it gets really weird—"

"Here's where it gets weird? I can't think of a sitch where you being stalked through the halls of school and on the bus by an actual ghost can get weirder."

"I think I know who she is."

"Come again?"

"I know who she is, or was, or whatever."

"Spill again," Ceci replied.

"Okay, so I had to spend the day with Nan after I got glutened—"

"Oh, Nan!" Ceci interrupted. "How is sweet Nan? I miss her and those snickerdoodles she makes—"

"Ceci, focus!"

"Right, yeah, sorry, go on."

"I saw a plaque in the hallway at school. There weren't many deets other than her name, year she was born, and the year she died." A shiver ran up her spine with the last few words. She couldn't believe she was talking about a poor girl who never made it past the age of fourteen. Nova saw Ceci get her own chill; her friend shivered and closed her eyes.

"That's so sad. What's her name? I mean, to have the

actual name of the ghost haunting you? That's pretty rare stuff there, Nov."

"Yeah, I guess. Her name was Evelyn Chambers."

"Evelyn Chambers," Ceci said, drawing out the words like she was letting her mouth and her mind try the name on.

"So, I have her name: bonus points. The next day with Nan—who by the way is doing okay, not great, and far past her snickerdoodle-making days but maintaining—I asked her if she knew who Evelyn Chambers was and how she died."

Ceci put her hand to her heart at the news of Nan's condition. Sadness etched on her forehead as she flashed a quick frown.

"Evelyn was allergic to peanuts, and she died of shock after accidentally eating something with peanuts in it."

Ceci's eyes widened. "Didn't she have one of those pen things? You know, like Heidi Gentry carried around all the time? Heidi was allergic to bee stings, but I think it's the same thing, right?"

"Yeah, for Heidi it was bee stings; for Evelyn Chambers it was peanuts. And there was an EpiPen, but she didn't get the injection in time. I don't know why. Nan said EpiPens were brand-new when Evelyn died. Like she was the first kid at the school who had one."

"Wow, that is horribly sad."

"Yes, it is."

"But why you? You've only lived in that town for a couple of months. Why would some girl who died decades ago be following you around?"

"I'd like to know the answer to that question."

As they spoke, Ceci opened her tablet lying on the bed next to her and searched the name Evelyn Chambers and Westland Park Middle School. There was a long pause in the conversation as Ceci's eyes grew wide and shock spread across her face.

"Well, I have one theory," she said.

"Really?"

Ceci turned her tablet to face her phone so Nova could see what she dug up.

"Look at her, Nova!" Ceci exclaimed.

"Yeah, okay, I've seen her before—on the plaque, online, in the creepiest bathroom in the world."

And you didn't see the resemblance? You two could be twins!"

Nova scoffed. She'd noticed the girl had similar features but didn't think they resembled each other that much.

"Nah, I don't see it."

"Don't be thick, Nov. Evelyn Chambers looks so much like you it's creepy. Even in the fuzzy black-and-white image, you can see the similarity. I bet if this was a better picture, you'd look even more alike."

"If you say so," Nova replied, scanning the image closely.

"But there's more!" Ceci said, closing the tablet.

"More?"

"Yes, you two have something else in common."

"When did you become such an expert on Evelyn Chambers?" Nova asked.

"The peanut allergy, the celiac disease ... two conditions, both involving food—" Ceci dragged the words out slowly.

"That's kind of a stretch."

"Maybe, but you got anything else? Maybe she haunts all the new kids and is waiting around for one to believe her and connect."

"I don't know about that. I mean, Ayden is kind of a

new kid. He hasn't said anything to me about seeing a ghost in the school."

"Have you asked him? Have you told him about your experiences?"

"Well, no, but—"

"Well, there you go! You don't know if he's seen the ghost or not. Maybe you should ask." Ceci was nodding her head in a manner Nova would expect from her mother. Something Nova had seen plenty of times before. Despite her friend being a little ditsy sometimes, she'd always given good advice and was the most intuitive person Nova knew.

"Honestly, I can't believe you haven't said anything to him yet. Maybe he can help you. At least you'd have someone to confide in. I mean someone there, who gets to see you every day."

Both girls locked eyes with each other. Both sets of eyes were fighting tears.

"I miss you so much," Ceci said, brushing a tear off her cheek.

"I miss you too," Nova replied.

"My mom drones on and on about how lucky we are that we can FaceTime each other. If I hear her mention long-distance charges and snail mail one more time…"

The sadness passed as Nova giggled. She could imagine Ceci's mom's voice saying those exact things.

"I think you need to tell your new not-boyfriend—" She waited for a response from Nova and raised her eyebrows repeatedly, as if she was waiting for some juicy piece of gossip.

"We're just friends," Nova replied.

"You keep telling yourself that; maybe you'll believe it."

"Friends! One hundred percent friend zone," Nova assured her.

"Well, if I were you, I'd tell my friend. It can't hurt."

Nova wasn't so sure about that. While she and Ayden were tight, they'd only known each other for a couple of months.

"Maybe. I'll think about it."

There was a knock at Ceci's door, and then Nova heard Ceci's older brother's voice.

"Wait for me to answer before you walk in, loser!"

"Whatever, loser. Mom said to come downstairs for dinner," Ceci's brother said. His voice sounded so much deeper since she had last seen him. He sounded more like Ceci's dad now.

Ceci looked back to the screen with an exaggerated eye roll.

"You're so lucky you're an only child," Ceci said. "Gotta bail. Keep me in the loop and tell the boy! Take my advice!"

"Maybe," Nova replied. "Talk to you later!"

"Ciao!" Ceci said a second before the screen went blank.

As Nova lay in bed that night, she played out different scenarios in her mind about how Ayden might respond if she told him she was visited frequently by a ghost. She wasn't sure how long she lay there, awake, her mind tossing and turning more than her body. Finally, she reached the decision to confide in Ayden and deal with whatever fallout came from it. As she was beginning to nod off, certain of her decision, she heard the familiar creaking of the hallway floor. Mom was home. She drifted to sleep to the quiet sounds of her mother readying herself for bed.

Chapter 14

The next morning passed slowly as Nova was eager to get to lunch so she could tell Ayden about Evelyn Chambers. When the lunch bell rang, she waited for him at their table. Her lunch sack remained unopened, and her phone screen locked, as she nervously tapped her fingers on the table while her eyes followed his slow crawl through the lunch line. Butterflies flitted anxiously in her stomach as he approached. When he set his tray on the table, before he was even seated, she blurted out the question.

"Do you believe in ghosts?" Immediately she felt foolish as her well-practiced mental script flew out the window.

"Good day to you too," he replied, a playful grin on his face.

"Sorry, I'm really glad to see you. I need to tell you something."

"Hit me. Oh, and yeah, I do believe in ghosts, so…" Ayden puckered and twisted his lips, lifting one shoulder before leaning in encouraging her to continue.

A bit of the tension that gripped her shoulders melted.

He believed in ghosts, which was as good a start as she could imagine.

"Okay, this is going to sound weird. I mean—" Despite having gone over her story a dozen times since she woke up, she found herself suddenly lost for words.

"Weirder than flat-earthers? Weirder than the Mandela Effect? Trust me, if you ever go down the Mandela Effect rabbit hole, be prepared to have your mind blown!" Ayden finished up by raising his hands to his head, his fingers uncurling from his hand to simulate an explosion.

Nova rolled her eyes. She wanted to laugh at her friend's antics but was hyper-focused on telling him everything she knew about Evelyn Chambers and her belief that the girl was haunting her.

"Yeah, I'm sure it's all very fascinating, but I have to get this off my chest."

"Sure, sure, sorry, straight face, serious mode activated. Go!"

Nova took a deep breath and closed her eyes, trying to remember how she intended to start. She started with day one.

"On my first day here, I was in the hallway alone, doing the whole locker thing."

Ayden leaned in, his lunch forgotten, intently focused on Nova's words.

"I heard a voice. I mean, it wasn't coming from another classroom or anything, it was right behind me. I got super cold and then someone said, 'I've been waiting for you.'" She paused for a moment, collecting her thoughts and waiting for Ayden to laugh. He didn't, so she pressed on.

"All kinds of things have started to happen since then. Some unseen person sits next to me on the bus every day. And then..." She paused, trying to think of the right words. "I've seen her. The day I got sick, she followed me into the bathroom and asked me to help her."

"So let me get this straight. Someone has been creeping on you in the school and on the bus?"

Nova nodded her head.

"And this has been going on since day one—day one—and you're just now telling me?"

"Well, yeah. I didn't want you to think I was some weirdo."

"Nova, brace yourself, I know you're a weirdo and I think I would have liked you even more if you told me you had your own ghost. I mean, seriously, that's some pretty cool stuff there. I don't know why you would keep this from me. I'm, I'm, well—" Ayden fluttered his eyes and tried his best to produce fake tears while fanning his face. "The betrayal."

Seeing that Ayden was willing to go down the ghostly path with her, Nova loosened up entirely. Her shoulders relaxed, and she finally broke into her lunch. She dipped a carrot stick into her hummus and told Ayden everything about being haunted by Evelyn Chambers while crunching away at her food.

She finished telling Ayden all she had to say just as the bell rang. Neither of them flinched this time, perhaps having grown used to the bell, but more likely because they were so immersed in conversation. They got up and walked toward the exit together, Ayden stopping to dump his tray and then depositing it on a growing pile of empty others.

"I must say, I'm intrigued," Ayden said. "FaceTime me tonight. We'll have a brainstorming sesh."

"Sounds good! Thanks, Ayden," she said. She was so relieved to have someone on her side, she didn't even dread the bus ride home with her invisible seatmate.

No sooner had Nova gotten off the bus and unlocked the door to the apartment than she heard her FaceTime alert. She dropped the mail, her backpack, and her water bottle and fumbled in her pocket for her phone. It was Ayden.

"You are never going to believe this," he said eagerly.

"What?" Nova took a few steps and collapsed on the couch.

"I can't tell you," Ayden replied.

Nova shot up from the couch.

"Can't tell me? How can you start a conversation like that, only to go directly to not being able to tell me? Not cool, Ayden!"

"I know. I know. I'm sorry, it's just, well, I don't want to get caught."

"Get caught? I'm sorry, but you have me confused." Nova flopped back down on the couch.

"Yeah, so, I did a little eavesdropping," he said, lowering his voice to a conspiratorial whisper, sneaking glances over both shoulders.

Nova was getting annoyed now. Ayden was FaceTiming her from his bedroom. Who did he think would be sneaking up on his conversation? Normally Nova got a kick out of his flair for melodrama, but when it came to this subject, she found it irritating.

"Eavesdropping? On who?" she asked.

"I can't say." Ayden sunk lower in his chair; his body hunched over his phone as if it were a test he didn't want anyone cheating on by copying his answers.

"Ugh, Ayden," she exclaimed. "Why did you even call me if you could only say that something big happened, but you can't tell me about it?"

"Well, I told you I would call. I couldn't exactly not call. That'd just be rude."

"Not any ruder than blasting that you have something amazing to tell me, only to say not now."

"Yeah, I can see that." He straightened himself in his chair and shrugged a shoulder. "You have to trust me on this."

His head snapped in the direction of his door. Nova heard a voice calling him in the distance.

"Look, I gotta bolt, basketball practice," he said. "Try to get to the cafeteria as quickly as you can tomorrow. I'll spill it all then. I can't talk about it here in my house, where someone could overhear me. Literally, I would be grounded until I graduated college."

"Okay, if you say so. I still think you're doing me dirty," she replied. "I'll just be here dreaming up all kinds of ideas about what could have you so jacked up. No worries."

"Don't waste your time," he said. Ayden turned his head away from the phone and yelled, "Coming, Dad!" Turning back to Nova, he said, "No way in a million years would you guess what info I have, but trust me, it is epic and might reveal some clues about Evelyn Chambers."

The call disconnected. Despite Ayden's insistence she not dwell on the subject, she did little that evening besides dwell on it. At bedtime, her mind was still swimming with unknowns and more questions about what Ayden might have uncovered. She fell into a troubled sleep plagued by images of Evelyn Chambers. She came to when she heard the creaking floorboard and bolted upright. Hearing her mother go about her routine soothed Nova and she quickly fell into a deeper sleep, thankfully free of visions of Evelyn Chambers.

Chapter 15

The next day, nothing happened fast enough for Nova. The bus ride seemed longer than usual. Her classes dragged on for hours. By the time the lunch bell rang, she wasn't hungry for anything more than Ayden's news. She took her lunch sack with her to her third block to avoid having to fight the crowds in the hall at lunchtime. Minutes before the class was over, everything was packed up and ready for her to dash out of the classroom.

She made it to the cafeteria in record time, only to find that Ayden had beaten her there. He sat with a home-packed lunch, which was unusual for him. He urged her to hurry by waving to her. Before she lowered herself onto the bench, he spoke.

"You're never going to believe this," he said, sounding out of breath.

"I'll never know if I can believe it or not if you don't just spill already."

"Okay, before I start, you have to promise me you won't tell anyone, and I mean anyone, about this information and how I came to know it," he whispered. She had never seen a more solemn expression on his face. Nova understood he was completely serious, a drastic change from his usual laid-back demeanor.

"Ayden, I promise on anything you want me to promise on. I'm about to burst with curiosity, so please, tell me!" She anxiously tapped her fingers on the table, and scooted up in her seat, glancing around to make sure no one was within hearing distance from them.

"So, yesterday, I had to stick with my mom after school. We were going to meet up with my dad for dinner."

"Okay," she said, wishing the tiny details could be dispensed with, so he would get to the meat of the story.

"I was waiting in her office, but she must've forgotten I was meeting her there. I overheard her and Ms. Merritt talking about the school nurse. I've only seen the nurse a couple of times because she left for medical leave shortly after my mom and I started here."

"Yeah, I heard something about her absence. But what does the school nurse have to do with Evelyn Chambers?"

"Well," he said, his eyes darting around the room, searching for anyone in hearing range, "she's not out having a baby or her hip replaced or anything like that." His tone and behavior spoke to some enticing revelation that was going right over Nova's head.

"So what? Who cares what old people are off doing—"

"Hear me out," he pressed.

Nova leaned in closer.

"They said she snapped!" he said, slapping both hands onto the table, eyes wide.

Nova just sat there, waiting. He visibly deflated, the look of shock slowly wiped clear off his face, replaced by disappointment as if he didn't understand why she wasn't reacting as he had to the news. She fixed him with an icy stare that pleaded for elaboration.

"I still don't get it," she said.

"Okay, so maybe that wasn't the best part of the story but get this." He leaned across the table, moving as close to Nova as his lanky body allowed. "She snapped right here at the school. Ms. Merritt tried to keep it hush-hush, but some students saw her. She told my mom the whole story while I was right inside her office!"

"Well, that's messed up, but I don't think you should be so judgmental about mental illness." Nova closed her eyes, her hands clenched into fists. She willed herself to take a deep breath as she thought about episodes her father had in public as well. Her mother tried to shield her from most of the fallout, but she felt the change in people: how they treated her, the looks of pity on their faces. It angered her that those people didn't know her dad like she did. Didn't know he loved playing Scrabble with her, or that he taught her how to play a few songs on the ukulele. They never knew how great a dad he was when his mind was stable.

Nova felt tears gathering in her eyes and fought hard to keep them contained. She blinked madly and looked away from Ayden.

"No, that's not what I meant," he pleaded. His eyes told her he knew he'd crossed a line he wasn't aware existed.

Nova cleared the sadness from her mind and focused on getting the conversation back on track.

"It's what she said the day she…" he said. Nova could tell he was searching for words that wouldn't upset her. "She kept repeating that Evelyn wouldn't leave her alone. That she had to get out of the school because Evelyn Chambers was following her through the halls."

His final words hung like a heavy cloud over the table. Nova sat motionless, trying to absorb his words and their meaning. Someone else had been haunted by Evelyn

Chambers, a grown-up at that. Ayden sat quietly. The two said nothing for several minutes.

"So," Nova started, still searching for the words she wanted to say. "She saw Evelyn Chambers, here at the school?"

"Yes! Her husband had to come up and get her. Ms. Merritt said she was hysterical. She locked herself in her office and screamed for the girl to leave her alone."

Nova's head tilted to one side as she found herself deep in thought. She'd certainly felt like running and hiding when Evelyn showed herself. Now she had proof of another person going through the same thing.

"Well, that's sad."

"I know, right? She's at Health Springs Manor now."

"What's that?"

"It's a ..." Ayden started in his normal voice, "mental health facility." He finished in a whisper so quiet she read his lips more than heard the words.

"That's even sadder," Nova replied.

"It really is. And get this ... Merritt joked about it."

"What? How does someone joke about something like that?"

"I don't know. She laughed off the whole thing, saying all teachers and school workers wish they could check themselves into Health Springs Manor sometimes. It was weird."

"Very," Nova replied.

"My mom ditched her after she said that and came into her office. I slipped my AirPods in and pretended I was into some TikTok."

"Nice."

Silence fell between the two again as Nova let the news wander through her mind.

"So, what are we supposed to do with this knowledge?

How does this help my predicament? Not to be completely selfish, but I thought you had news I could use to get Evelyn Chambers to leave me alone."

"Since we don't have anyone else we can talk to about it, I think we should go visit Nurse Brumley."

"Oh, no, Ayden. I don't think that's a good idea," she snapped, shaking her head and finally breaking into her lunch sack. That seemed to remind Ayden they were there to eat. He reached into his brown bag and pulled out a bag of chips.

"Why not?"

"It seems horribly rude. She doesn't know us. How would we even get in? It sounds risky."

"I hear you, but before Ms. Merritt started joking about it, she told my mom that Mr. Brumley, Nurse Brumley's husband, calls her sometimes and asks if any of the students would like to visit her. She said he thinks being around kids would do her some good."

"Hmm," Nova said, nibbling on a carrot stick as she let the news roll around her thoughts, waiting to pick up a reason for going along with Ayden's brazen plan.

"She wants visitors, Nova. We could be those visitors," Ayden said, flinging a pointed finger back and forth from himself to Nova.

"I don't know. I'd need to think about it for a bit," she replied.

"Don't take too long. I have a plan."

"Why does that not surprise me?"

"Next Monday is President's Day—"

Thanks for the history lesson," Nova said, trying to lighten the mood.

"We don't have school that day..." he said, stretching the words as if giving her time to make some kind of connection.

"Great!" she replied.

"Guess I have to spell it out to you," he said, clearly exasperated with Nova.

"Yes, I think you do need to spell it out to me. Maybe give me a PowerPoint presentation, because I'm not sure where you are going with this."

"Does your mom work that day?"

"My mom seems to work every day these days. She even picks up shifts on her days off." Nova let those words fade, quickly lowering the volume of her voice; saddened by the reason why her mom was working so often.

"My mom has to work that day too. Staff team building or something like that, whatever that means."

"So we've established our parents won't be around. What's next, mastermind?"

"You have a bike, right?"

Nova looked at him as if the question was the most absurd thing she'd ever been asked.

"Perfect," he said, ignoring her sarcastic expression. "My house is about two miles from Health Springs Manor. We have the day free. You bike over to my place and from there, we pay Nurse Brumley a visit."

"Just like that? We walk in and say we're complete strangers, there to see the unfortunate Nurse Brumley?" Nova was exasperated by the entire conversation and began stuffing her lunch items, most of them uneaten, back into her bag. "You're like a one-man think tank, huh?"

"Not complete strangers," he said. "Former students, as in the type of people her husband wishes would visit her. Smell what I'm stepping in?"

"Gross!" Nova said, wrinkling her nose in disgust.

"Sorry, but you see what I mean?"

"Yeah, I get it. I still think it's, I don't know, bold."

"What if she has answers for you? Seems to me she is the only person who knows Evelyn Chambers as well as you do."

"I guess," she said slowly. "But what if we get in trouble?"

"For giving Nurse Brumley what she wants? I don't see how it could go wrong. Trust me, I'm smooth, I got this."

"Smooth? Whatever!" Nova laughed with an eye roll. She knew if anyone could pull off such a daring scheme, it would be Ayden.

"Come on, you in? I don't want to do this alone."

"Fine, I'm in."

Chapter 16

Nova and Ayden straddled their bikes at the top of a hill. Below them sat the sprawling Health Springs Manor. Nova felt as if the building were glaring at her, daring her to come closer and listen to its secrets. There was only one secret she wished to hear today. She glanced at Ayden, who gave a nod, and the two pushed off, sailing down the winding road.

The front gate was open and if it weren't for the smattering of life mingling outside on the grounds, the foreboding facility would be the stuff of haunted house nightmares. But it was an unseasonably warm day, and the sun shone on the dew-coated impeccable landscaping. Caregivers in mint green lab coats tended to individuals and small groups of people, some of whom sported their robes or hospital gowns, while others wore casual street clothes. Squirrels flitted their tails and chased each other across the grounds and into the trees. All and all, it looked like a pretty decent place to go if you needed a break from life. Maybe a place like this could have benefited her dad, if only he'd agreed to get help.

"That's her, over on that bench," Ayden whispered as he pointed to a woman sitting by herself at the farthest reaches of the gated gardens. "She's alone."

"Perfect! Hopefully, no one will even notice we're here."

The two had discussed as many scenarios as they could dream up on how to gain access to the fragile Mrs. Brumley. Never had they imagined they wouldn't have to put any of those dodgy plans into action.

"It's now or never," Ayden said, getting off his bike and propping it up against the gate. He unzipped his backpack and pulled out a small bouquet.

"Wow, you thought of everything," Nova said as she propped her bike up against the gate as well.

"This isn't my first rodeo," he replied. "It's my second."

Nova couldn't help but laugh despite the nervous energy coursing through her veins.

"Had to seem legit. Two kids bringing flowers to their school nurse makes things more believable. Who brings flowers when they are breaking the rules?"

Nova took a deep breath, and Ayden swung his arm out in a gesture telling her to go first.

As they moved across the vast lawn, Ayden took the lead and walked coolly to where the small woman sat. Nova was anything but cool. Her eyes darted in all directions, fully expecting someone to approach and chase them away. But no one seemed to notice the two as they drew near the woman.

"Nurse Brumley," Ayden said softly. "Do you mind if we have a seat?"

The woman looked up at them. Her eyes were crystal blue, but empty, lost, as if awakening from a heavy sleep.

"These are for you, Mrs. Brumley," Ayden said, taking

a seat next to the woman and laying the flowers in her lap. He didn't wait for her to respond to his question.

"I'm Ayden Simmons, and this is Nova Eckley. We're students at the school," he offered.

Nova stood next to him. She tracked Mrs. Brumley's gaze as it shifted slowly from his face to hers. Nova thought she saw a flash of concern, fear almost, in the woman's eyes. It only lasted a second, not long enough for her to be certain she saw it at all. Then the woman's face softened, and she shook her head as if shaking a thought out of her mind.

"You can call me Nicole. We aren't at school, so Nicole is fine. For a minute I thought you were her," Mrs. Brumley said. Her tone matched her sleepy demeanor. She noticed the flowers in her lap and brought them to her nose, inhaling deeply, eyes closed. A slight smile touched her lips. The three sat in silence for a while before Mrs. Brumley opened her eyes. It seemed as if she had forgotten her visitors while she breathed in the sweet scent of the bouquet.

"You look like her, you know," she said to Nova. "But you aren't crying. Every time I see her, she is crying."

Nova couldn't think of a response and was grateful when Ayden chimed in.

"Who are you talking about, Mrs. Brumley?"

Slowly, almost reluctantly, the woman's eyes shifted back to Ayden.

"Evelyn," she said. "Evelyn Chambers."

Ayden's back straightened, and Nova took a seat on the other side of Mrs. Brumley, fearing her knees might give way if she didn't. Earlier that morning, they discussed several ways to coax the school nurse toward the subject of Evelyn Chambers. Both were shocked the woman jumped right into the topic. Things were going far more smoothly than anticipated, which unnerved Nova even more.

The two were so intrigued and hopeful at Mrs. Brumley's willingness to speak to them, they didn't notice the orderly approaching until the woman's shadow slid across the trio.

"Excuse me," the orderly snapped. "You two mind telling me what you are doing here? They aren't bothering you, are they now, Mrs. Brumley?"

Ayden stood and took the lead again.

"Sorry, Ms.—?" Ayden scanned the woman's lab coat for a name tag.

"Shanice Brown," the woman replied, putting her hands on her hips. "But you can call me Nurse Shanice."

"We're students from the school where Mrs. Brumley works. We thought we'd come to visit since we didn't have school today. All the students miss her." The words slid out of his mouth effortlessly. If Nova hadn't been in the know, she would have believed him. In reality, neither of them had attended the school when Mrs. Brumley dispensed medications and handed out ice packs and Band-Aids.

The woman's stance immediately softened. A wide smile spread across her face.

"Well, aren't you two the sweetest things ever?" she gushed. "You're supposed to check in up at the front desk, but I'll let it slide this time."

Nova could feel the heat rising up her neck, as her cheeks burned red. Ayden remained calm and cool.

"Oh, sorry. We were so excited to see her out here enjoying this nice weather, we forgot all about checking in."

Nova could do nothing more than avoid eye contact with the woman while she nodded her head in agreement with her friend.

"Mr. Brumley always asks if any of the students come to visit his wife. He'll be tickled pink when I let him know about you two. Mm-hmm, tickled pink." The woman's bright smile never left her face.

"It's the least we could do. She means so much to the school."

"You brought flowers too," Shanice exclaimed. "How sweet! Well, I'll let you get back to your visit. You let me know if you need anything, anything at all. She has about an hour more before she needs to go in for lunch."

The woman turned to leave, talking to herself as she walked away. "Just the sweetest. And they say kids are only interested in themselves and video games these days. If that just doesn't prove…" She turned and waved at them one last time as she made her way to another patient.

Nova feared the interruption might throw Mrs. Brumley off the track she had so willingly led them onto. Of course, Ayden was three steps ahead of her and forced the conversation right back to where it had gotten derailed.

"So, Evelyn Chambers," Ayden prompted.

"Yes, she is sad," Mrs. Brumley replied. A tear slid slowly down the woman's face.

"Why is she sad?" Ayden asked.

"Well, she died, you know," Mrs. Brumley offered, as she reached into the pocket of her cardigan and pulled out a tissue. She wiped the tear away and gently rubbed the tissue between her fingers as she continued, wearing it so tiny bits of white fluff fell onto her lap. She didn't seem to notice.

"She wasn't supposed to die. It was just a prank, and she wasn't supposed to die. We didn't know, didn't know it would go so wrong." Mrs. Brumley had her eyes fixed on something Ayden and Nova couldn't see. She was reliving a moment from long ago and was more present in it than she was in the one she shared with the two teens right then.

Silence fell over the group. As the minutes ticked by,

Nova hoped Ayden would again move the conversation along. Instead, she ended up blurting out a question.

"Do you see her still, Mrs. Brumley?"

The woman's eyes came back into focus, and she shifted her gaze to Nova.

"Because I do. I see Evelyn Chambers all the time."

"You see her too?" Mrs. Brumley said, grabbing Nova's hand. "I thought I was the only one. Ever since I started working at that school, she followed me. I tried to ignore her, but she wouldn't leave me alone. Finally, I … I—" Sobs overtook her. Her body shuddered and her shoulders hitched. Nova squeezed the woman's hand and fought tears of her own. It was clear Mrs. Brumley was deeply troubled, even more so than Nova, over the sightings of a long-dead girl.

"It's okay, Mrs. Brumley," Nova said. "We aren't here to judge. We want to help. Help you, help her…" Nova trailed off as Mrs. Brumley tried to regain her composure. She took a deep breath and blotted her eyes with the tissue. Ayden was visibly relieved that Nova had taken over when things got emotional. He looked to Nova, his eyes wide, telling her without words how incredible this revelation was.

"I transferred out of that school after she died. Wish I had stayed away for good. But I needed a job. At first, I thought I was managing, as if I could get past it all. I was wrong. I couldn't take it anymore," Mrs. Brumley said, sniffing and dabbing her nose with the soaked tissue. She put the used tissue in one pocket and retrieved a fresh one from the other.

Ayden found his voice again. "What did you mean, a prank?"

"It wasn't my idea. We knew she was allergic to

peanuts. Neither of us knew it was deadly, though. We thought hives would be the worst reaction. We were so wrong." Mrs. Brumley began to sob again. "It was only half a peanut, one tiny piece. She put it in her cupcake while Evelyn wasn't looking. Not even a whole peanut, just half."

Nova and Ayden eyed each other over the woman's slumped figure. Nova knew he was thinking the same thing as she was. His expressive face told a story. Neither of them could believe the school nurse would give up so many telling details about the death of Evelyn Chambers.

"I tried to go for help. But she wouldn't let me. She said we'd get in too much trouble. And then she left me there. Me, alone, with Evelyn. I couldn't believe she was slipping away." The woman's eyes took on that faraway gaze again. "I thought if I held her, I could keep her there. If I didn't let go of her, I could save her, stop her from leaving."

Now Nova was crying. The pain the woman was reliving was as visible as if it had a life of its own. It was something felt so strongly that it kept poor Evelyn Chambers tethered to this world. What did the ghost girl want? Revenge? Redemption? It made sense to Nova that Mrs. Brumley would be haunted. She played a role in poor Evelyn's demise.

But why Nova? What had she done to attract the girl's spirit?

"I sat on that floor for the rest of the day. I didn't let go of her, not until the final bell rang. She was cold when I laid her down. I ran. Left her there alone on the cold floor," Mrs. Brumley continued, startling them both with her sudden words. They rushed out of her like waters breaking a dam.

"I was so afraid. I've never forgiven myself. How could

I be such a horrible coward? I'm so, so sorry. So sorry," the woman said. She grabbed Nova's hand again, squeezing it tightly, and looked directly into Nova's eyes. "It's why I became a school nurse. To make up for that one horrible thing. I thought a career helping kids might help me forgive myself, but I was wrong."

Nova looked over Ayden's shoulder and saw Nurse Shanice making her way back to them, a look of concern etched on her pleasant face.

"The nurse is coming back," she said to Ayden.

"Mrs. Brumley, who were you with? If it wasn't you, who thought of putting the peanut in her food?"

Nova was grateful for Ayden's quick thinking. She was too bogged down by the woman's grief and the implications of her story; she didn't think to ask such a pertinent question. Nurse Shanice was now mere steps away from them. The urgency was palpable.

"I can't tell," she whispered. "We swore to never tell on each other. We made a pinky promise."

"Mrs. Brumley," Nurse Shanice said, her voice tainted with worry. "What's the matter, dear?"

Nova set her expression to show confusion and was glad to see Ayden followed suit.

"We're so sorry, Mrs. Brumley," Nova said to the sobbing woman. Then to Nurse Shanice, she added, "We didn't mean to make her cry."

"That's alright now, children. She's been a touch emotional since she arrived here. I'm sure it was nothing you two did, but I am going to have to ask you both to leave now. My apologies."

"Oh, right, sure." Ayden stumbled on his words as he and Nova got up from the bench.

Mrs. Brumley seemed to have disappeared inside herself again. She took no notice of the nurse, nor of the rapid departure of the teens. Neither of them offered any parting words to Mrs. Brumley as they hurried back toward the entry gate.

Not a word was spoken as they biked their way back to Ayden's house.

Chapter 17

Nova and Ayden sat together on the porch swing at the Simmons's house. The swing swayed slowly, and when it threatened to stop, one of them would push off gently with their foot, setting it in motion again.

"That was intense," Ayden said.

"Seriously."

"Remember, we can't say anything to my mom about our little expedition today."

"Yeah, I get it. I won't tell anyone," Nova assured him. "But what do we do now? Where do we go from here? I mean, what do we do with this information?"

"Your guess is as good as mine. Maybe that's all she wanted. Evelyn, that is. Maybe she wanted someone to know it wasn't an accident."

"I don't know. Something tells me that isn't all she needs."

"Guess you'll find out soon," Ayden said.

"How?"

"Well, you mostly see her at school, right?"

"Yeah, and on the bus." Nova never told Ayden she had seen Evelyn Chambers right here, at his house.

"So, if you don't see her at school, like, say for the rest of the week, maybe then you'll know she's moved on, or whatever."

"Maybe. At least I can hope so. But something feels unfinished to me. Like there's more to the story."

"I don't know how you do it. I mean, if I had some ghost kid popping up on me all the time, I think I'd check myself into Health Springs Manor too."

"It isn't fun, trust me. At least she hasn't followed me home. If she stays at the school and on the bus, I know I can relax sometimes.

"At least you have that, I guess," Ayden said. "I'll be right back. I need a snack. My mom bought some gluten-free trail mix. Want some?"

"Sure, thanks."

"I'll ask what time she plans on taking you home," he said, getting up from the swing and making his way to the door.

The swing lurched erratically when he rose but soon settled and almost came to a stop. Nova sat alone, her legs crisscrossed underneath her. She watched a daddy longlegs walk awkwardly over the welcome mat on the porch. An angry, dark cloud engulfed the sun, while far in the distance a low grumbling of thunder echoed through the sky.

Nova felt the temperature drop significantly and chalked it up to the impending storm. The porch swing settled to an imperceptible quiver. She closed her eyes and listened to the soft chirping of birds nested somewhere nearby. A sudden jolt set the swing in motion again, and she jumped.

"Not funny, jerk!" she yelled, wondering how he had

snuck up on her without hearing him. Ayden wasn't there, but the swing still rocked back and forth with more force than was possible. A chill ran up Nova's spine, and she jumped up from the swing. Her eyes darted about the space, looking for the person who sent the swing into action. There was no one there, no one she could see anyway.

Slowly she walked backward, eyes now never leaving the swing. The back of her leg connected with a cushioned chair that sat opposite it. She allowed herself to be drawn into the chair as she watched the swing. It never slowed until she heard Ayden approaching, yelling to Nova when it abruptly came to a complete stop.

"Can you get the door?"

Nova jumped up and reached for the door, her eyes still locked on the motionless swing. The icy stagnant air was gone in an instant.

"We're gonna have to eat these snacks on the road," Ayden said, exiting the house with his arms full of water bottles, soda cans, a bag of chips, a box of cookies, and a bag of trail mix. "My mom wants to leave now so she can get you home before this storm hits."

Nova was ready to get off the porch and away from the one other place where the ghost of Evelyn Chambers could find her. She jumped up and grabbed her backpack. Her bike was already loaded in the back of Mrs. Simmons's truck.

Mrs. Simmons clucked when she and Ayden climbed into her vehicle.

"Child, if you spill any of that in my truck..." She didn't indicate what she would do but continued shaking her head as they backed out of the drive.

"This break in the cold weather has been a nice surprise," Mrs. Simmons said. "But winter temperatures are following this storm in. Another false spring. It's a shame, really. My tulips are already starting to sprout. Fingers crossed they survive."

Nova wasn't listening to Mrs. Simmons, but she nodded her head. Ayden was oblivious to his mother's words, too busy stuffing his face with cookies. When they pulled in front of Nova's apartment, Ayden hopped out to help her unload her bicycle.

"You're getting Cheeto dust all over my handlebars," she said, as he set the bike down.

"You're welcome," he joked. "But for reals, the bag said gluten-free right on it. Makes my heart smile knowing you can indulge in the joy of the Cheeto."

Nova took the bike and waved at Mrs. Simmons. She rushed to her apartment door, unlocked it, and pushed the bicycle in with her. Once inside, she flipped on the lights and hung her bike on the hooks in the cramped entryway. Her mom didn't get President's Day off, so the apartment was empty. An angry crash of thunder shook the building. The storm had arrived.

She didn't have any homework, so she played Minecraft for a while. But the game couldn't distract her mind from reliving her encounter with Nurse Brumley. She opened a new tab and googled the name, Evelyn Chambers. She found the girl's obituary and read it. The picture of Evelyn brought tears to Nova's eyes. The girl was beaming, the warmth of her smile electric. Even the dog she held in the photo was smiling. Evelyn had been an only child. She played soccer and took gymnastics and loved to sing.

Warm tears slid down Nova's face as she grappled with the reality that Evelyn Chambers missed out on so much. She would never have a boyfriend or learn to drive, never graduate high school or get her first job. Knowing what she did now, made the girl's death all the more tragic. A prank thought to be innocent, that went so horribly wrong. It wasn't fair.

There was a newspaper story marking the tenth anniversary of Evelyn's death. Evelyn's parents stood next to a man in a suit, who was identified in the article as Mr. Mastin. He was the school's principal at the time the memorial plaque was placed in the school trophy cabinet. The somber expressions on all of their faces spoke to the sadness of Mr. and Mrs. Chambers.

Next, she searched Mrs. Brumley. Her social media pages weren't private, so Nova scrolled through her photos. Many pictures appeared to have been taken at the school within the past few years. She and Ms. Merritt were kindred spirits. At Field Day, they sported matching jogging suits and ran at the back of a pack of smiling chil-dren. On Pajama Day, they wore their hair in curlers and donned matching robes and slippers. For Halloween, Ms. Merritt dressed as the Wicked Witch of the West while Mrs. Brumley wore the familiar blue gingham dress, her hair in long pigtails, as she carried a basket that held a stuffed animal that looked like Toto the dog. Mrs. Brumley looked happy in each picture, but as she looked closer, something caught Nova's eye.

In the background of the Field Day picture stood a child. A child whose face was distorted, like her face was smudged out of the photo. The child wasn't dressed in shorts and running shoes like all the other kids. These kids frozen in running poses, every one of them, one leg lifted, arms pumping, fists clenched. All of them, that is, except the smudge-faced girl. She wore a dress, knee socks, and stood still, both feet firmly planted on the ground, hands at her side.

Nova clicked on the picture of the two on Pajama Day.

There, again, was smudge-face girl. A handful of kids stood with the principal and vice principal. All the kids were dressed in pajamas of all manners—except for the girl. She stood between Ms. Merritt and Nurse Brumley, her back straight as a rod in her dress and knee socks. The two women did not appear to notice the creepy photo-bomber that stood next to them.

She quickly found the Wizard of Oz photo. This shot was taken from above, as if the photographer stood on a high ladder to get as many kids in the picture as possible. Firefighters, Batmans, princess tiaras, and poodle skirts filled the space. All of their faces looking up, their laughter caught in perfect frame.

Nova scanned the image, her face close to the screen, eyes squinted. Maybe the girl wasn't in this shot, she thought, but then she saw her. Standing at the back, no costume, almost transparent, her face smudged over like she was shaking her head wildly when the picture was snapped.

It was all too creepy for Nova to look at anymore. She was about to close her laptop when a thought struck her. She scrolled back through her history until she found the picture where the plaque was being presented. She wasn't surprised to see the girl again. This time, she didn't stand in the back. The three people in the photo stood immediately in front of the trophy case, leaving no room for another person. But in the reflection of the glass, there she was … almost a shadow, a shadow with no face.

A shiver took over Nova. Quickly, she took screenshots of each of the images before she shut the laptop. The pictures of the girl were too much for her to look at any longer, but she wanted Ayden to see them, mostly to confirm what she saw was real and not a figment of her imagination.

Night's darkness settled in the sky. The angry storm chased the spring-like day away with thunderous booms. Cracks of lightning split the sky and lit the room in blinding flashes. Nova yawned and stretched. Usually, she loved a good thunderstorm, but now as she sat alone in the small apartment, knowing her mother wouldn't be home for hours, she wished the storm would burn itself out soon. Nova went to her bedroom and pulled a nightshirt out of a drawer. Violent wind whipped the saplings outside her window. Their scant limbs, barely showing buds of green, having been tricked by the false spring, clamored against the glass as if begging to be let in.

Nova went to the bathroom to get ready for bed. While brushing her teeth, she scrolled through TikTok videos. As she turned to the sink to spit, the floor outside the door let out its familiar creak. She froze, wanting to call out for her mother, hoping she had left work early due to the storm and made it home to find her daughter in the bathroom, dutifully readying herself for bed. But Mom would make her presence known. At this early hour, knowing Nova wouldn't be asleep yet, she would have swung the front door open and announced herself; she wouldn't sneak in. The bathroom lights flickered before turning off, swallowing Nova in darkness.

Frozen in terror, she couldn't force herself to find the light switch. The thin line under the door revealed the shadow. This was no play of the lightning—someone stood outside. As if to make certain Nova knew she was not alone, the person on the other side of the door turned the doorknob.

A horrifying doubt raced through her mind. *Did I lock the door?* The answer came loudly as the knob twisted back and forth, the entire door shaking violently.

She held still as a statue, not allowing breath to escape

her lips. Her heart pounded against her ribs so loudly, she was certain whoever stood outside the door could hear it as well. The floor squealed again, jolting Nova into action. She backed up slowly against the wall. She was trapped.

Her only option was to distance herself from the door and whoever was out there trying to break in. She considered getting into the bathtub, as if the thin shower curtain could offer her more protection from the angry intruder, but feared she would make too much noise. Under the threshold, she saw movement. Two shadowy blurs, a pair of ghostly feet, shuffled impatiently on the other side of the door. The blood that pounded through her veins turned to ice. She was frozen in fear but needed to do something to chase the invader away. With her eyes tightly closed, she dug deep and screamed.

"Go away! Please leave me alone!" Once the words escaped her throat, she was reduced to heaving sobs.

On the other side of the door, the shadows held still for a moment before disappearing. The lights popped back on, blinding her. Nova's knees buckled and she slid to the cold floor of the bathroom. Tears spilled down her face. She'd never been more afraid of anything in her life.

————

"Silly girl, why are you asleep on the floor?" Her mother's kind voice awakened her. Nova jumped up and threw her arms around her mom. "Oh, sweetie, you are shaking. What's got you so scared?"

Nova couldn't think of what to say. She threw out the easiest response she could think of.

"The storm. It kind of freaked me out."

"Oh, my, yes! It was a doozy! Why don't you climb into my bed? We'll have a slumber party in my room."

Nova felt too old to share a bed with her mother, but who would ever know? She knew she wouldn't be able to sleep after what she had experienced. This whole day was one terrifying event after another. She walked into the hall, leaving her mom to go through her bedtime routine.

As she took her first step, her bare foot landed on something hard and icy cold. She lifted her foot and bent down to pick up what she stepped on. She squeezed her eyes tightly shut, and when she opened them again, she didn't understand what she was holding. It was a key. An old-fashioned key, like the ones she saw in fairy tales. The key was glazed in cracked rust and a layer of dust.

For reasons unknown to herself, she wanted to keep the key secret from her mom. She ran to her room and put the key in the small pocket on the front of her backpack. Then she grabbed her pillow and dashed to her mother's room, where she settled into the mattress.

As she listened to the noises Mom made while getting ready for bed, she contemplated telling her the truth. The thought of her mom's reaction was almost as frightening as the experiences she was having. She knew there was no way any of it would make sense to her mom, and she couldn't stand the fear it was certain to bring to her. Mom would undoubtedly believe that she was losing her daughter the same way she lost her husband.

If she made her mom feel that way, Nova wouldn't be able to live with herself.

Chapter 18

The next morning her mother rose early to get ready for work. Nova stirred but remained under the covers, feeling the safest she'd felt since her dad went away. Her mom sang an old pop song while she showered. It was still dark outside, but the only sign of the previous night's storm was a steady drip of water from the broken gutter on the roof.

"Good morning, sleepyhead!" her mom said as she returned to her bedroom in her fluffy robe, towel-drying her hair. "How'd you sleep?"

"Better than I thought I would," Nova said as she sat up in the bed and stretched her arms over her head.

"Well, that's good. You've never been afraid of storms. Are you sure there wasn't something else last night that spooked you? After all, you locked yourself in the bathroom."

"No, maybe it's because this was my first storm in this house, and I was alone."

Nova regretted what she said immediately as she watched her mom's concerned look turn to sadness. Her mom's face said so much in that moment: guilt, anger, sorrow. The girl jumped out of bed and went to her mom, wrapping her arms around her and pushing her face into the soft robe that smelled like nothing else but her mom. No one scent could be picked out, but to Nova, it was the most familiar aroma in the world.

"But now that I've survived my first storm alone here, I am sure it won't happen again. I don't know why I was being such a baby." She delivered this line in the most cheerful voice she could muster. Her mom squeezed her tight.

"It's okay to be afraid, Nova," she whispered. "These days I'm more afraid than I have been in my whole life. But we have each other. You and me against thunderstorms, mean girls, and everything else."

Her mom gave her one little squeeze, before releasing Nova from the hug.

"My supervisor is who I am most afraid of! I can't be late. Shake your tail feathers and get yourself ready. The bathroom is all yours."

In the bathroom, Nova gazed at herself in the mirror. She looked exhausted and was glad Mom hadn't noticed the dark circles under her bloodshot eyes.

Back in her bedroom, she got dressed. Next, she went to her backpack. With shaky hands, she reached for the small front pocket, unzipped it, and put her hand inside. She didn't know which would be more frightening, finding the key or finding nothing. She didn't have to ponder long. Her fingers brushed against the cold metal. A wave of relief flowed through her; she hadn't dreamt up the key, but it was still a bit terrifying to know that it was there.

On the drive to school, Nova stayed quiet. She knew that somehow Evelyn Chambers had been in her apartment last night, intent on handing over another clue. Her mind struggled with how to pull off her next task. She needed to find the lock the mysterious key belonged to—a mission made more difficult because she had absolutely no idea where to begin looking. The school building was old, but the key looked ancient.

She was eager to talk to Ayden over lunch. Maybe he would have a logical take on the whole matter.

"Have a great day, sweetie!" Mom said as they pulled into the drop-off lane. "I'm sorry I can't be home when you get there. I love you."

"No worries, Mom," Nova replied. "I'm getting the hang of this latchkey kid thing. Love you too!"

The morning passed uneventfully. Nova kept the key in her sweater pocket, her fingers absentmindedly tracing the outline of the rusty relic. She took notice of every door and scanned the keyhole in each of them. The only ones she saw were modern locks, none of which looked like they might be opened with the skeleton key.

At lunch, she rushed to her table. Ayden was already there, waiting for her.

"Whoa, what happened to you?" he asked as she took a seat across from him.

"What do you mean?" Nova replied, smoothing her hair.

"You look like you haven't slept."

"Oh, thanks for noticing." She unpacked her lunch sack in a huff. "For the record, I haven't slept, at least not well. Catching my Zs while being haunted by the ghost of a girl who won't leave you alone isn't great for one's beauty rest."

"Yikes! Sorry."

"It's okay," Nova replied, the tension leaving her shoulders. She took a deep breath, closed her eyes, and reached into her pocket. "So, up until last night, I've only seen Evelyn in the school and on the bus. My apartment was my safe place—*was* being the buzz-word." She hated leaving out the sighting at his house but didn't want him to be burdened with the knowledge.

"She followed you home?" Ayden asked, his lunch sat forgotten in front of him. His wide eyes focused solely on Nova.

"Yeah, and she left a little something too." Nova withdrew the old key from her pocket and slid it across the table.

"Whoa, what? Like she popped up and handed you this antique?"

"Not exactly. I didn't see her. I heard her. But I didn't know it was her, not really. I mean, I was totally freaked out. I fell asleep on the bathroom floor waiting for my mom to get home."

Ayden picked up the key and turned it over and over in his hand, nodding his head while Nova spoke, clearly hearing what she was saying, but mesmerized by the old key.

"Anyway, my mom found me there. I was so embarrassed. When I left the bathroom, I found this on the floor outside the door. It wasn't there before. It had to have been Evelyn who left it for me. As far as I know, she's the only one haunting me right now."

Ayden put the key down and pushed it back across the table.

"So, have you told your mom about any of this?" he asked.

"Are you kidding? No way! My mom's got enough to worry about. The last thing she needs is to think her kid's mind is slipping." A part of Nova wanted to tell Ayden about her dad, about his illness, and why it was more important for her mom not to know about Nova's troubles with seeing and hearing things. But she couldn't bring herself to do it.

"Fair enough," Ayden replied. "So what do you think this key means? Do you recognize it?"

"No, I was hoping you might have some idea. I've looked at every door I've passed today. I mean, I figure it has to belong to a door here at the school, right?"

"Yeah, this school is a fossil. I can't think of anyplace else as old as this place."

"I don't know how I can figure out where the door is that this key unlocks, but if Evelyn followed me all the way home to make sure I got it, it must be important."

They both jumped as the bell rang, signaling the end of lunch. Quickly, they gathered up the remnants of their meals and made their way to the trash cans near the exit of the cafeteria.

"I'll see if I can get any info from my mom," Ayden said to her as they parted ways.

"Cool, thanks," Nova said. "See you in fifth hour."

In her next class, the teacher called her up and asked her to take some files to the front office. Nova's face flushed at the request, and beads of sweat sprang forth on her forehead. She'd been so successful at avoiding being alone in the hallways, but now her luck had run out. Silently, she took the files from the teacher. Mr. Parker was oblivious to her reaction as she slowly made her way to the door. She stopped and peered out the long window that ran down the length of the doorway. There was no one there.

She pushed through the door and picked up her pace, eager to get to the office and safely back to her classroom again. As she made her way past the hallway that was under construction, motion caught her eye. Her mind screamed at her to keep her eyes focused on the office ahead, not to chance a glance down the hall, but her instincts betrayed the urgent warning—and she turned her head to look.

It was Evelyn.

The girl stood in the middle of the mouth of the corridor. She motioned with one arm, beckoning Nova to come to her. Nova froze in her tracks, and a blast of cold air filled the hallways. She squinted her eyes shut and silently counted to ten, hoping Evelyn would be gone when she opened them.

Evelyn wasn't gone, but she had turned her back as she walked away from Nova. After a few steps, the girl turned and motioned again with her hand, urging Nova to follow her.

Nova's heart galloped inside her chest, and she felt powerless to resist the girl's summoning. She carefully stepped over the construction supplies and ducked under scaffolds, barely taking her eyes off the girl's twitching, shadowy figure. At the end of the hall, Evelyn stopped and looked back at Nova before she ascended a set of stairs that were tucked away, shaded in darkness. Nova turned away from the stairs, too afraid to follow the girl into the unknown.

In a flash, she changed her mind. Evelyn's pull was too strong. It was as if the ghost girl wormed her way inside her mind forcing her to not run away. Nova turned and peered into the lightless space. It was so dark, the stairs appeared to vanish into nothingness after the first three risers. Gathering her courage, she placed her foot on the first step and reached for the railing with a trembling hand. The handrail felt as cold as ice. Before she lifted her foot to the second stair, a booming voice behind her echoed through the corridor.

"Hey, kid!"

Startled, her heart froze and missed a beat, and she

dropped the folders. She looked down, hoping the papers hadn't spread all over the floor. Thankful they remained sealed, she bent to scoop them up quickly.

"You can't be down here," the man said, his burly shape moving closer to her. "It's dangerous. I'm not wearing this hard hat as a fashion statement."

"Right, yeah, sorry," Nova pleaded as she made her way back down the hallway. "I got lost."

"Sure, 'cause this hallway looks like it's fit for kids. Go on now, get out of here. And don't let me catch you down here again."

Nova skirted around the man's large figure. He smelled of sawdust. Before she made it to the main hallway, she stopped to see that the trophy case had been cleared out. Evelyn Chambers was forgotten to the school now, the last hint that she had roamed these halls gone.

She turned to look back down the corridor. The construction worker was digging through a box of something, mumbling under his breath, seemingly having forgotten about Nova. Standing right next to the man was Evelyn. Nova was certain an expression of sadness flashed upon the girl's face before she blinked out of focus and disappeared.

Chapter 19

When she reached the choir room for the day's last class, she walked directly to Ayden.

"I saw her again today. She led me to a staircase," Nova said in a conspiratorial whisper. "I don't know where the stairs lead."

"Well, why didn't you follow her up them? Maybe she was taking you to the door that key unlocks."

"Yeah, that's what I was thinking, but I got caught before I could follow her up."

"Caught? Caught by who? Ms. Merritt? Did you get detention?"

"No, it was a construction worker. He didn't bust me, but I don't know how we are going to get to that staircase again. And I have no idea where it leads."

"I can try to get some intel from my mom. But that doesn't include a hall pass to the haunted hallway of reno nightmares."

Mrs. Hastings interrupted their conversation. "Good afternoon, friends." The teacher gave a stern but good-natured nod to Nova, directing her to her place on the risers without drawing too much attention to her. "Don't forget, tomorrow is our first Pizza-Wednesday of the second half. I hope you all can make it. Caitlyn's parents have graciously agreed to provide the pizza." As she spoke, she wrote the details for Pizza-Wednesday on the white-board before turning back to the class.

"Alright then, let's get started. Vocal warm-ups—"

At the end of class, Ayden met up with Nova and the two walked to her locker.

"Pizza-Wednesday is the perfect opportunity for us to check out that hallway and see where the stairs lead," Ayden said.

"What is Pizza-Wednesday?"

"Um, exactly what the name implies. On Wednesdays, the choir and drama club kids meet in the choir room and eat pizza. It even has its own Insta handle, at-pizza-dash-wednesday, all lowercase," he said enthusiastically.

"Wonderful, a pizza party. There is literally nothing more triggering for a kid with celiac than a pizza party." Nova rolled her eyes. "The worst!"

"Oh, yeah, right. Sorry," Ayden replied. "Don't they make gluten-free pizza? I know I've seen it."

"Ah, yes, sauce and cheese bubbling atop a cardboard 'crust'; personal pizza sized for the price of an extra-large supreme 'normal' pizza, with the added anxiety of cross-contamination by pepperoni."

"Sounds delicious," Ayden said apologetically. "Well, tomorrow we won't be eating pizza. I mean, I won't either. But it will make for the perfect cover. No one will expect us to be in the cafeteria, and they won't miss us in the choir room. Plus, everyone will be eating lunch at that time, even the construction crew. My mom is always complaining about the crew taking extended lunch breaks. Pizza-Wednesday to the rescue!"

"Yay, Pizza-Wednesday," Nova said, the words wrapped in sarcasm as she waved her hands.

"That's the spirit," Ayden said. "Pun one-hundred-percent intended. Get it? Spirit, ghost, boOOoOo."

"You're the worst," Nova said, unable to hide her laugh.

On the bus ride home, Nova felt the presence of Evelyn Chambers sitting beside her. She held tightly to the belief the girl meant her no harm. The incident in her home bathroom had terrified her. It was the scariest thing she'd experienced in her life. But she believed that Evelyn was desperate and needed to get her attention. Frightening as it was to know she was in the presence of a dead girl, Nova began to think of Evelyn as a friend. She felt sorry for the girl as she thought of all the things she had missed out on since her life was cut short. Thoughts of Evelyn's final moments consumed her mind sometimes, shrouding her in sadness.

The next morning, Nova woke from a troubled sleep. All night she tussled with what-if thoughts of how the day could play out. Would this be the day she could free Evelyn from the confines that held her here seeking help? Nova was resolute—she couldn't let fear keep her from doing what she knew needed to be done.

Ayden was waiting for her outside the school, shifting his weight from foot to foot, blowing into his cupped hands, then rubbing them together vigorously. Winter blew through again, chasing the fool's spring away for a few more weeks. As Nova approached her friend, her eyes were drawn to the top-floor windows, wondering if the answers were locked away up there and whether the key would allow them to uncover what Evelyn wanted so badly for them to find.

She saw Evelyn standing in a gable window. When

their eyes met, a chill snaked down Nova's spine and fear gripped her in its icy hand. Nova shook it off, pushed the panic down, and ran to meet Ayden.

"Today's the day," she said as she joined him at the top of the stairs.

"I thought you weren't that into Pizza-Wednesday," he said. His face twisted into an exaggerated mask of confusion.

Nova had to laugh. There was no one else she'd rather have at her side while she faced such a menacing task. Ceci was even more of a chicken than she was. If she alone held the responsibility of solving the mystery of why Evelyn Chambers was attached to this school, it would never happen. She admired Ayden's bravery and humor and gave him a gentle shove through the door.

Once inside the school, the calm she had felt in the courtyard slid off her like a snake shedding its skin. Her resolve was challenged when she saw Ms. Merritt cheerfully speaking to Caitlyn Rogers in the foyer. She realized Ms. Merritt likely never kept her promise to speak to Caitlyn about the cookie incident. A flush of anger flooded her, and she forced herself to take deep breaths and let it go. Her focus needed to be placed on the matter at hand—Evelyn, not Caitlyn.

The two made their way down the hall when Nova stopped short. The kid behind her slammed into her, and she turned to apologize. Ayden seemed oblivious that Nova wasn't walking beside him and continued to move with the crowd for a few steps. His head protruded above the group of junior highers, and Nova saw him glance down to where she'd been by his side, and then he halted as well. The group parted ways around his lanky form, only to merge back together as they passed him by. Ayden turned and walked against the tide of kids back to where Nova stood.

"What's up?" he asked. "Why'd you stop?"

Nova's only reply was to point in the direction of the hallway that was under construction. A thick milky plastic wall now blocked the hallway from view. To Nova, it also meant the hallway was obstructed, and that didn't fit into their plan.

"They barricaded the passage," she muttered when she finally spoke. Her eyes met Ayden's, her expression helpless.

"Let you in on a little secret," he replied. "See that construction worker?"

Nova nodded and tracked the man with her gaze as he approached the newly hung plastic sheeting.

"Patience, grasshopper. Watch and learn."

The man carried his hard hat under his arm and balanced a donut on top of a paper coffee cup. When he reached the wall of plastic, he set his lunch box down and tugged on a seam running down the middle of the heavy sheath. He turned and backed into the opening he'd created, skillfully keeping his coffee cup upright, the donut motionless as he bent to grab his lunchbox. He disappeared behind the wall of plastic.

"Behold, the wonders of Velcro," Ayden said, leaning toward Nova's face, his eyes wide in mock amazement.

"Wow, you've unlocked some level nine construction know-how. Where'd you learn that?"

"There are parts of my past that I cannot speak of."

"Right," Nova laughed.

"For real," he replied. "If I told you, I'd have to…"

The first bell rang and the two jumped, then turned to notice the crowd in the hall was thinning.

"You'd have to what? Kill me?"

"Worse, I'd have to admit that I used to be Bob the Builder's biggest fan."

"You're such a complete dork."

"Maybe, but you love me. Meet you back here at lunchtime for hashtag pizza-wednesday Ghost Hunt."

With his parting words, her humor evaporated, replaced by a heavy darkness. She dreaded what she would face that day. There were so many things that could go wrong. She didn't even know if their plan was a solid one. But it was all she had at that moment, so she knew she had to go through with it. This train of thought held her so deep in its grasp that she didn't notice the tardy bell as she reached her homeroom and took her seat just before the blaring chime ended.

Her morning classes crawled by slowly, and Nova couldn't focus on anything. In Algebra, when the teacher asked her what she got for question eight on their pop quiz, she fumbled with her papers and mumbled the incorrect answer. Hushed giggles made a wave through the classroom, but she was too consumed with anxiety to care.

Chapter 20

Lunchtime finally rolled around, and Nova intentionally lagged behind the sea of students making their way to the cafeteria. She scanned the group for Ayden but didn't see his tall frame above the crowd. When she was confident the hall had cleared and no one was paying her any mind, she quickly walked to her locker. She was glad she'd left the lock open this morning, saving her precious seconds. Even when she wasn't on edge with trembling hands, she struggled with the old padlock. She opened the locker and shoved everything into it except for her phone and the key; then made her way back down the empty hall, hugging the bank of lockers believing she was less conspicuous.

As she drew near the foyer hallway, she heard voices and ducked into a classroom alcove. It was Mrs. Hastings and Ayden.

Nova pushed her body as far against the classroom door as possible but realized Mrs. Hastings was distracted by her phone. Ayden's long arms carried a stack of pizza boxes so tall, only a kid his size could manage.

"Thanks so much for carrying these pizza boxes,

Ayden," Mrs. Hastings said, not looking up from her phone. "The delivery man was almost fifteen minutes late. I planned to have all these boxes out and ready before lunch hour started."

Ayden spotted Nova and mouthed words to her that she couldn't make out.

"No problemo, Mrs. Hastings," he said, sharply turning his attention back to his teacher. "Not like I had anything better to do." His gaze returned to Nova, his expression conveying apologetic helplessness.

Nova faced the terrifying reality that she was alone on this mission. It took her mere seconds to decide she would proceed without Ayden. She only hoped that determination would stick with her when she reached the dark staircase at the end of the hall.

She slid out of her less-than-ideal hiding spot and tiptoed around the corner. A group of men emerged from the plastic wall as she drew closer. Each of them carried an old-fashioned metal lunch box and thermos. Nova didn't know where the men went to eat their lunches, and she hoped none of the workers stayed behind. There was no time to ponder this; the longer she remained in the open, the more likely she was to get caught. She pulled open the Velcro seam and slipped into the corridor.

The space was dim. Stale sunlight struggled to penetrate the grimy windows. A thick layer of white powdery grit coated everything, giving the appearance of a landscape recently dusted by snow. She saw motion at the end of the hall. It was Evelyn. The girl was looking at Nova, one hand raised, beckoning Nova to follow her. Nova strode toward the girl, believing she appeared more self-assured than she was. She fought her instinct to turn and run and willed her breathing to calm, her pulse to slow, and her body to stop trembling. All she wanted to do was turn back and hurl herself through the plastic door.

Her shoes left footprints in the thick grime. When she reached the halfway point between the mouth of the hall and the staircase, she stopped and looked back over her shoulder. How she wished Ayden would show up. She needed his encouragement. She needed his bravery. Nova turned back to the staircase in time to see Evelyn Chambers turn and disappear up the steps.

Nova took a deep breath and slowly stepped forward, then quickened her pace. When she reached the dark stairway, she stopped and took another glance over her shoulder. From this angle the corridor looked much longer, seeming to stretch even further before her eyes. She took a deep breath and turned back to the stairs. Next, she pulled her phone from her hoodie pocket and turned on the flashlight. The passage was so dark, it stole the light from the flashlight, gobbling it up in inky blackness. The only way to tell how high the stairs reached was a thin gash of illumination at the top, beyond the impenetrable gloom. She raised a foot and set it down on the first step. A cold blast of energy pushed her, prompting her forward with its icy hands.

She focused the flashlight on the risers as she climbed the heavy metal stairs. The world was draped in deafening silence. The only noise was the hollow echo of her footfalls as she ascended in the darkness, and her heartbeat, pounding quickly inside her chest. As she drew near the beam of light, she realized it was coming from a crack under a doorway at the top of the stairs. The light had a welcoming warmth that seemed to embrace her and calm her fearful mind.

Slowly, she waved the flashlight over the door. It was old and made of solid wood, not like the hefty steel doors throughout the rest of the school. The beam of her light fell upon the tarnished doorknob. Encased in an ornate faceplate was a keyhole. She knew this was the lock the mysterious key would fit, and she willed her hand to stop shaking as she used her flashlight to focus on the lock. The weathered key slid into the keyhole with ease, as if it had been waiting for its companion. She turned the key and heard the internal mechanisms of the lock come to life, creaking and clicking. Her attention was so focused on the lock and on keeping herself calm that she didn't notice another beam of light penetrate the darkness before landing on her form, creating a shadow of herself on the door.

"Psst! Nova!"

Ayden's voice shattered the eerie quiet, causing Nova to startle. She was sure her heart stopped beating for a moment, and her stomach clenched tightly, threatening to spill into her throat. A breathless gasp escaped her mouth. She turned quickly, the key dropping from the keyhole as she did. She thrust the beam of the flashlight onto the ground as she heard the key clatter through the risers. The key bounced from surface to surface with a tinny clink. Nova's spirit weakened with every clattering bounce before the key landed with a dreadful clank somewhere far from her reach or sight. Frantically, she swept the beam of the light through the open risers in a desperate attempt to find the key, its beam powerless to pierce the shifting darkness.

Ayden was running up the stairs to her and she let out a wretched wail. The key was gone. How could she have come this close, only to have hope slip through her fingers?

"Ayden!" She jerked her body toward her friend, feeling an angry heat pulsate from her face. "What are you doing? You made me drop the key!"

"Are you serious? I'm sorry, I wanted to help you out.

We have to get out of here! The workers are making their way back into the school right now. If we don't leave, we'll get caught."

Desperation landed on her shoulders like a heavy weight. She was so close, and now she'd lost the one thing she believed held the chance for her nightmare visitations by a dead girl to end. Hot tears slid down her face; she was unable to control them.

Ayden grabbed her hand.

"We have to leave, now!"

Nova resisted as he pulled her down the stairs, but it was useless. If she got caught she might never get the chance to return to the door, perhaps pry it open and see what was behind the door Evelyn Chambers so fiercely wanted her to see. She gave into Ayden's insistent guidance and allowed herself to be drawn toward the landing. When her feet hit the floor, she tried to pry her hand from Ayden's grip.

"Give me a minute to find the key," she pleaded.

"Are you crazy?"

His words stung like a slap to her face.

Above them, the old wooden door began to vibrate, as it shook in its casing. The sound of fists battering the solid door echoed down the passage. The thunderous noise gave life to the thick dust blanket around them, stirring the debris into a cloudy mass. They shielded their eyes and pushed through the fog. When they made their way through the dust cloud, they turned back to the tunnel of stairs in time to see the powdery residue twist itself into a spinning funnel, before abruptly losing all energy. The cyclone disappeared and its particles drifted to the floor like falling snow.

Shadowy movement drew their attention to the head of the hallway. Rousing laughter exploded on the other side of the plastic wall. They were trapped, but the two pushed forward, hunched over, Nova's hand in Ayden's as they side-stepped the tools and equipment. They were close to the opening when the scratching sound of Velcro separating echoed in the hall. The teens pressed their bodies behind the trophy case and tried to quiet their heavy breathing. Their eyes wide, darting madly as if looking for someone to help them.

A beam of light from the separated plastic sheet fell upon the hallway, landing mere inches from Ayden's feet. The bright ray threatened to expose their hiding place. Nova squeezed her eyes tightly closed and held her breath. She felt Ayden's respiration come to a gasping halt as well. Just then a familiar voice beyond the draped covering rang down the foyer hall.

"Gus! Men, can you spare a moment please?"

It was Ms. Merritt, her form silhouetted on the plastic sheath as she approached the crew.

"Good afternoon, gentleman. Your lunch breaks become longer with each passing day. I'd hate to have to bring it up to your foreman."

There was a mumbling of responses from each of the men. Apologies and groans Ms. Merritt paid no mind to.

"I'll trust you will be more considerate of the time from here on out."

"Yes, ma'am," the group murmured in unison.

"Now, I would like us all to meet in my conference room. The district's security team is here to go over camera placement. They would like to install cameras throughout the building while they're here. Of course, that means you all might be working in close quarters given the state of things. We need to work together to make the installation seamless. You can leave your stuff here in the foyer. It shouldn't take long."

Before much longer, the shuffling sounds of the men unloading their lunch boxes ceased and silence filled the space. Nova knew this was their chance to escape the corridor without getting caught and wasted no time clamoring through the opening. Ayden followed so closely behind her she could feel his breath on her neck.

The air in the foyer was lighter, and the dreadful sense of claustrophobia diminished in the brightly lit entry. Still, Nova felt defeated and hopeless. She had blown her chance to get to the room she knew held secrets she needed to uncover.

"I lost the key, Ayden," she said bleakly. "Now we'll never know what Evelyn Chambers wants me to see."

"Don't be such a downer. We'll figure something out." His tone wasn't reassuring. "Right now, we have to get to class before the tardy bell rings. I don't think my nerves could handle a sit-down with Ms. Merritt this afternoon, or worse, my mom!" Ayden shivered at the thought.

"Well, I'd rather not be followed around by a ghost for the rest of my days."

Ayden rolled his eyes. "Let's not be so overdramatic. We'll figure something out. Now, go—get to your locker. We'll talk later."

Ayden was gently guiding her toward her locker, but she pulled away from his nudging hands and walked on her own, dragging her feet, her shoulders slumped in defeat.

Later that day on the bus, Nova felt the familiar pressure in the seat next to her. She was almost glad to feel the girl's presence. Since her abysmal fail with the key, she feared Evelyn Chambers would give up on her. She turned to face the invisible passenger and whispered, "I'm sorry."

Chapter 21

The next day the concert choir began rehearsals for the spring concert. Nova tried her best to suppress her gloomy disposition, but Caitlyn's behavior weakened Nova's resolve. The girl stepped on Nova's song parts and upstaged her, her voice too loud, drowning Nova's vocals. The two weren't harmonizing; they were battling.

Nova's frazzled nerves didn't help the situation. She held angry words in, tightly clenched behind her teeth until she couldn't fight them any longer.

"There's no fortissimo symbol on the sheet music, Caitlyn," she growled.

"Excuse me? Are you really trying to critique my singing and knowledge of how to read sheet music?"

Mrs. Hastings noticed things weren't off to a good start with the two girls and intervened.

"Nova, Caitlyn, why don't you two take five," she said. "Get a drink of water or something."

Nova was grateful for the chance to step away from the frustrating rehearsal. She moved behind the acoustic curtains, where she slumped to the ground and fought back tears. She wished her dad was here. He always had answers for her and knew the best way to handle any situation. Since starting school, her focus was fitting in and figuring out why she was being visited by Evelyn Chambers. She had given little thought to how much she missed her father. When memories of her dad tried to push themselves to the front of her mind, she quickly pushed them away, dashing the chance for her to accept and grieve his absence. It was too much for her to face.

Now, however, it was impossible to repress thoughts of him. He would know exactly how to handle Caitlyn. And while she doubted she would tell him about Evelyn Chambers, just having him with her would be the boost she needed, the encouragement she knew would help her through the struggles she and her mom were facing. Then again, neither of them would be dealing with so much change if he had never left.

She heard footsteps approaching and rose quickly, dabbing her face and smoothing her hair. Before the curtain was pulled back, she heard Caitlyn's voice.

"Nova," she hissed. "Where are—"

Caitlyn pulled back the curtain and the glare of the stage lights blinded Nova briefly. She closed her eyes, and colors bloomed and flashed in her vision. Before Caitlyn finished her question, Nova felt something brush swiftly by her ear. Something that fell from the catwalks far above the stage. It hit the polished wood floor with a hefty clank. Nova opened her eyes slowly to not be blinded again. She glanced down at her feet and saw the key. She knew it was the same skeleton key she dropped into the darkness below the stairwell the day before. Magically, it appeared from the sky. She bent to grab the key, but Caitlyn swooped in, snatching it up before Nova could lay a finger on it.

"It's dangerous to throw things on stage, Nova. That's stage etiquette one-oh-one."

Nova couldn't think of a response. She needed to get the key away from Caitlyn, who held it up to the light, examining it from every angle.

"I wonder what this is?" the girl questioned out loud to no one. "Maybe a prop from an old performance. It looks ancient."

"It's mine," Nova said, reaching for the key. As her fingers drew near, Caitlyn jerked the key out of her reach.

"Not so fast, Nova. What would you need with a rusty, old skeleton key? Maybe I should turn it in to Mrs. Hastings."

"No, Caitlyn!" Nova found a voice she didn't recognize as her own. "Give it back! I said it was mine!"

Caitlyn's eyes met Nova's and the girl shrunk away, willfully handing over the key to Nova, then withdrawing quickly. She didn't know what had possessed her to be so forceful. Her strong reaction and overwhelming emotions scared her. But as soon as she wrapped her fingers around the cold metal key, she felt a calm rush over her.

"Girls!" Mrs. Hastings yelled from the orchestra pit. "Your five minutes have now turned to ten. I need you center stage, pronto!"

Caitlyn turned quickly, looking eager to distance herself from Nova and the fiery tidal wave Nova unleashed. As she walked away, Nova saw the girl's perfect ponytail lift from her neck and her head snap back violently. Caitlyn grabbed the back of her head.

"Ouch!" she cried. She stopped and turned to Nova. The girls were too far apart for Nova to have been the person who pulled Caitlyn's hair. The girl said nothing more but dashed to the main stage without looking back again.

Nova remained alone in the depths of the curtains and turned the key over and over in her fingers. Now she knew the object was the key to learning why Evelyn Chambers was bound to this school. She looked up to the catwalk above her. It was empty, but she knew Evelyn was up there somewhere. She pushed the key deep into the back pocket of her jeans. Then, before moving the curtain aside and rushing back to join the class, she whispered, "Thank you!"

Caitlyn was a different person when the two belted out the words to their song. Her attitude a thing of the past, the girl was gracious and cooperative. Nova had never known Caitlyn to be so pleasant. It gave her hope the two could work together to make the duet magical. Nova's spirits were lifted as well, and Mrs. Hastings's smile beamed from the darkness of the orchestra pit.

Nova caught up to Ayden as the class was dismissed. She pulled the key out of her back pocket but kept a firm grip on it as she raised it to show Ayden.

"Look what I found!" she said, unable to contain her grin. "Or should I say, look what found me?"

"No way! How'd you get that?" Ayden reached for the key, but Nova snapped her hand away and secreted the key into her palm, balling it up inside her clenched fist.

"You wouldn't believe me if I told you," she taunted.

"Of all the things you've laid on me that I shouldn't believe, how could you doubt my willingness to accept every whack story you've thrown at me? I'm hurt," he said, grasping his chest and faking a swoon.

"Okay, fine," she conceded. "I found it backstage. Well, actually, it appeared backstage. It's hard to explain."

"Well, whatever happened, I'm glad you and the mystery key have been reunited."

"Me too," she said. "Now we need to come up with

another plan, and let's leave hashtag pizza-wednesday out of it!"

———

Nova's high spirits clung tightly to her. She welcomed the invisible companionship of Evelyn on the bus ride home. As they drew near her stop, she got a text from her mom.

> MOM: I finally have an evening off! Let's go out to dinner!

Nova didn't have the chance to reply as the bus squeaked to a stop in front of her apartment block. She jogged home, eager to have some time with her mom.

She burst through the door, dropped her backpack in the small entry, and ran to her mom who was standing at the kitchen sink. Nova wrapped her arms around her mom in a tight hug.

"Hey, you surprised me!" Mom said, laughing. She turned to hug her daughter back. "Someone's in a good mood."

"Yeah, my day started off sucky, but it got better."

"Well, that's nice. So, I heard of a new sushi place in town that has a gluten-free menu. Thought we could give it a try."

Nova loved sushi but couldn't hide the concern that washed over her face. Sushi restaurants could be expensive. They hadn't spent any money or eaten out, gone to movies, bowling, or anything else for several months.

"What's that look for? You suddenly not a fan of sushi? We can try something else, but our choices are pretty limited."

"No, it's not that. I could totally go for a Kyoto roll ... oh, and edamame." Nova could almost taste the briny appetizer. "It's just that, well, I mean, you've been saving money and I don't want to—"

"I see where you're going with this," Mom said. "But I've been working so many hours, and you've had to come home to an empty house, go to sleep without being tucked in. I think we both deserve a night out together." Mom's voice was shaky, and she was holding back tears. "It's sweet of you to be concerned, but I got this. I even called the place and grilled them about their prep process. They are really on top of things with a gluten-free menu and precautions in place to prevent cross-contamination. They passed my test with flying colors."

"Awesome! Now my mouth is watering!"

"I'm going to finish tidying up in here so if you have any homework, get it done. We'll leave around five-thirty if that works for you."

"Yep, I've got a little algebra to do, but it won't take long." Nova grabbed her backpack from the entry and went to her bedroom.

At five-thirty Nova put her schoolwork back in her backpack and opened her bedroom door to find her mom standing right outside her door, hand balled in a fist and raised, ready to knock. The two jumped in surprise and their laughter burst out simultaneously.

"Guess you're as ready as I am!" Mom said.

———

Nova and her mom sat in the dimly lit restaurant. The ambiance was relaxing, with red and black decor, bamboo, and a beautiful mural painted across one entire wall. They ordered two bowls of edamame and spoke little as they savored the salty soybeans. After the server brought their sushi out, Nova dove eagerly into her sushi roll. They even had gluten-free soy sauce, which was a bonus. Mom didn't touch her food. Her attention seemed fixed somewhere behind Nova.

"I'm glad this couple is finally leaving. She's been creeping me out all night. It's like she's fixated on you or something."

Nova skillfully placed a piece of sushi in her mouth with chopsticks and closed her eyes as she chewed slowly, relishing each exotic flavor.

"Don't look now," her mom said.

Nova turned her head and locked eyes with the woman. She almost spit out her bite and forced herself to swallow it before she choked on it. The woman staring at them was Nurse Brumley. The woman looked tired and frazzled, and her eyes widened when she saw Nova's face.

"I said, don't look!" Mom said. "Too late now. Do you know her?"

Nova's face flushed with alarm. She shrunk into the booth, attempting to make herself smaller. How would she explain to her mother that she knew the woman? Nurse Brumley and the man she was dining with got up from their table and made their way toward the table where Nova and her mom sat.

"Um, no, I don't 'know her' know her. She looks like the school nurse."

"The school nurse? Is she back at the school? I thought she'd been gone since before you started there. There's a rumor at work that she had a nervous breakdown." Her mother delivered the final words in a conspiratorial whisper.

"Yeah, uh, no," Nova stammered. She turned her head away from the couple and feigned an awkward interest in the bottles of condiments on the table, none of which she could even eat. If Nurse Brumley were to stop and talk to them, she'd be busted. She hated lying to her mom and as it stood, she convinced herself she hadn't lied. She'd just omitted a part of the day she spent with Ayden.

Sensing the couple had passed and were making their way to the exit, she sat up and turned back to her food.

"Well, what is it—yes or no?' Mom questioned.

"Oh, I, um I think I saw her picture on a wall in the school. Yeah, that's it." Nova wondered if her mom sensed the untruth, but she didn't have to worry. Mom was loading up a California roll with wasabi and pickled ginger.

"Oh, wow!" her mom said, her mouth still full of food. "This is divine!"

Comfortable the close call had passed, Nova relaxed and was able to enjoy her meal. In the back of her mind though, she wondered if Nurse Brumley was out of the hospital for good. She certainly looked different wearing jeans and a sweater, her face brightened by full makeup. Nova didn't think she'd notice the woman if they passed on the street. But she was certain Mrs. Brumley was aware of her presence. According to Ceci and the nurse, Nova bore a striking resemblance to the ghost who haunted the school.

Chapter 22

The next morning as she shuffled through the crowded hall on the way to first period, Nova glanced at some commotion inside the windowed front office. Under a banner that read "Welcome Back!" stood the office staff and some teachers. In the middle of the group, Nurse Brumley smiled and nodded uneasily, holding a vase filled with flowers. Somehow the woman homed in on Nova's presence and locked eyes with her. What should have been a passing glance was drawn out, making Nova uncomfortable. She didn't realize she'd stopped in her tracks, forcing groups of kids to part momentarily before closing back in on each other.

"Earth to Nova. Come in, Nova," a voice spoke to her, sounding as if it were coming from a distance.

Ayden stood in front of her, snapping his fingers in her face. Nova blinked rapidly and shook her head, bringing herself back to the moment.

"Wow, where'd you go just now?" Ayden asked.

"Did you see who's back?" Nova asked, motioning to

the office with her head, her eyes locked on Ayden's for fear of being drawn in by Nurse Brumley's stare.

"Oh, yeah, I forgot to tell you. Walk with me. We're both going to be tardy if we just stand here."

Ayden took a few steps away from Nova, then turned back and looked at her expectantly. His words sunk in finally and she hurried to join him.

"So, I have a plan," he said.

"What kind of plan?"

"Duh, a plan to get to the door that fits the key. What'd you think I meant? A plan to end world hunger? Keep up, Nova."

"Right, right. Sorry. We saw her at dinner last night."

"Saw who?"

"Nurse Brumley! Now who needs to catch up?" she said, throwing a gentle punch into his arm.

"Okay, noted. Actually, she plays into my plan."

"This should be good," Nova replied. They reached her locker, and she went about unlocking it and riffling through her belongings as Ayden spoke.

"So my mom has to stay late tonight. They are having a meeting with Nurse Brumley. Something to do with easing her back into the job or something. All lame and adulty. Anyway, if you can stay after with me, we'd pretty much have the school to ourselves while the faculty meeting is going on. I've already asked my mom. She said she could take you home afterward. I told her we needed to study for the science test."

"Um, yeah, sure. My mom works tonight. I'll have to text her, but there's no reason she'd say no."

"Cool, so it's a plan. Wait, you do have the key on you, right?"

"Oh, no!" Nova dropped her shoulders and set her face with an apologetic look.

Ayden's body language mirrored hers, the disappointment of believing his plan failed before it even began was evident. Neither noticed the thinning crowds in the hall as the start of first period was only minutes away.

"Just kidding, dork!" Nova laughed. She pulled her necklace out from her sweater. It held a locket that her dad had given her. Dangling next to the heart-shaped locket was the key. It was the safest place to keep it as she never took the necklace off. The skeleton key was a bit large for the chain, but she was comforted by the weight of the relic. She wiggled it in front of his eyes before tucking the silver bangle back under her collar.

"Not cool—" he started. His words were cut off by the screaming warning bell. They both jumped and the kids who remained in the halls scattered in different directions, bent on getting to their classes before the tardy bell rang.

"See you at lunch!" he said, darting away from her toward his first class.

———

When lunchtime rolled around, she found Ayden sitting at their table.

"You get the OK from your mom to stay after school?" he asked before she even sat down.

"Yep."

"Perfect! So let's meet in the library. The meeting doesn't start until four, so we need to make it look like we're settling in for a study sesh in case anyone, namely my mom, comes looking for us. When the meeting starts, we make our way to the forbidden hallway."

"What if the construction workers are still there?"

"You're funny. My mom says their workdays get shorter

and shorter. Says they always cut out before the last bell of the day assaults us all."

For the rest of the day, Nova's stomach was in knots. Not the kind that told her she might have ingested hidden gluten, but the kind that worried about all the things that could happen to keep them from reaching the door and finally learning what Evelyn Chambers wanted her to see. The timing of Nurse Brumley's return seemed ominous, spooky even.

At the end of the day, she found Ayden in the library. He'd gone so far as to set up a station for them on one of the back tables. She walked to where he waited and sat in the chair next to him.

"Don't forget to turn the lights out when you leave, Ayden!" the librarian yelled from the check-out desk.

"Sure thing, Mrs. Peters! Have a great night!"

"I expected the school to be empty by now," Nova said, her tone saturated in worry.

"Chill, there's always stuff going on here after dismissal. The important thing is that the people who could mess up our plan will be gone or preoccupied."

"I hope you're right. I feel like this key is trembling sometimes. It's in my head, I know. I just want this to all be over."

"You and me both, sister," he replied, cracking open his science book.

The two of them sat for what seemed to Nova like hours. In reality, it had only been minutes. She stared at the pages of the science book but saw nothing; read none of the words.

Finally, Ayden closed his notebook and stood up. He was tall enough to see over the bookshelves when he stood on his toes.

"Coast looks clear. I think it's time to solve this mystery, Watson."

Nova rose too and stuffed her belongings into her backpack.

"Um, I'm not Dr. Watson, I'm the Sherlock in this setup."

"How you figure?" he asked as they made their way toward the door.

"Actually, I don't think this is a Sherlock-Watson relationship," she replied.

"Yeah, I think you're right. It's more like, you're the Scooby to my Doo," he said thoughtfully.

"That doesn't even make sense, dork," she laughed, slugging him in the arm.

"Yeah, you're right. But it does have a nice ring to it. Mabel and Dipper?" he questioned. "Mulder and Scully? Phineas to my Ferb? Gumball to my Darwin? Mordecai to Rigby? Finn and Jake? I don't know..."

Nova was used to walking double time when she was with Ayden. With his long legs, his stride easily doubled hers. But this time she reached the end of the hallway and looked back before turning towards the front hall where they hoped to find Evelyn Chambers and saw Ayden lagging behind her, having slowed to a snail's pace while searching out loud for a fitting duo. Nova stood at the intersecting hallways: arms crossed, tapping her toes, and shaking her head.

"Hey, Patrick to my Spongebob, hurry up!"

"Wait up!" he yelled as he ran to catch up to her.

They passed through the hallways quietly, eyes darting about expecting someone or something to thwart their plan. The gymnasium was full of life and noise—the trill of the coach's whistle and the thunderous booms and squeaks of the basketball team practicing mixed with the spirited voices and claps of the cheerleading squad. Nova saw Caitlyn tightening her ponytail as they passed the gym's open double doors and elbowed Ayden.

"I hope she didn't see us," she whispered as they cleared the entrance to the gym.

"Right! She could Doofenschmirtz this whole plan."

"Wow, dude. It's time to let it go," Nova replied, stifling a laugh.

They reached the hallway that was closed off by plastic and paused, looking in every direction to make sure they weren't followed.

"Did you hear that?" Nova whispered.

"Hear what? Oh, sorry, it could be my stomach. I skipped my afternoon snack." Ayden replied, rubbing his belly.

"Get real, Ayden," Nova hissed. "I thought I heard something behind us."

"It's just the noise from the gym." Ayden spun in a circle before declaring, "Coast is clear."

Satisfied that her mind was playing tricks on her, Nova pulled the plastic apart creating a space just big enough for the two of them to squeeze through. Ayden followed and pulled the plastic sheeting closed behind him.

The hall was darker than ever as outside the afternoon sun was veiled by churning, gray storm clouds. Ayden turned on his phone's flashlight. The stark beam cut the darkness as ghostly dust motes shivered in its glow.

"You sure about this?" he asked.

Nova detected a concerning tremor in his voice.

"One-hundred-percent," she replied, pushing forward, hoping her voice didn't betray her fear.

Ayden took a deep breath and followed her.

"Ladies first."

"Who says chivalry is dead?" she whispered.

The distant murmur from the gymnasium was the only noise they heard. But Nova was certain if Ayden listened closely, he'd hear her heart thrumming rapidly and loudly inside her chest.

Nova navigated the construction debris, guided by Ayden's flashlight, and the two wound their way slowly toward the staircase. When they reached the landing, she could feel Ayden's body shiver. It wasn't cold in the hallway, but goosebumps rose on her arms. Ayden grabbed her hand, his fingers icy cold.

"We got this," she said. She didn't know if she was trying to assure Ayden or herself.

"There's a light under the door at the top," Ayden said.

"Yeah, I think that's where she—" Nova didn't finish her sentence. She was about to say 'lives,' but that wasn't right. There was no other word she could think of that fit.

"Lingers?" Ayden whispered.

While it sounded like a question, she was certain it was the best description. Still, she didn't reply.

Boldly forcing back a tidal wave of emotion—overwhelming fear being an understatement, mixed with hope, sadness, and more feelings than she'd ever felt—she climbed the first two steps. As she lifted her foot for the third tread, the light from Ayden's phone disappeared in a flash. She froze as the darkness pressed in on her. She squeezed her eyes shut, trying to force them to adjust quicker. The air in the tiny space was choking, the blackness complete. Disorientation swam around her, forcing her breath to quicken. Cold beads of sweat erupted at her temple and slid down her face and into her eyes. For a moment she believed she was alone, but she tried to calm her breath. Ayden was still holding tightly to her hand. He was gasping, on the edge of hyperventilating when Nova found her voice.

"Take a deep breath, Ayden," she whispered.

"I think my battery just died. But I swear it was charged. I'm not dumb enough to trek down this hall with a dying battery."

Her free hand fumbled clumsily in the dark, grasping blindly until she found his hand. She gripped it tightly.

"It's going to be okay. Try to calm down."

Ayden grabbed her other hand, and she heard him take a long, slow inhale. The air he blew out landed on her face. She breathed with him at least three times. When she sensed tension leaving his body, she tried to lighten things up the way he always did in stressful moments.

"What'd you eat for lunch today? Garlic and anchovies?"

She caught him mid-exhale. He couldn't control his laughter and spewed his breath out in a laugh.

"Nice one," he replied. His voice now calm, his breathing smooth.

"Ready?" Nova asked.

"As ready as I'll ever be," Ayden replied.

Nova tapped her foot, searching for the next step. The light above them, the thin line from under the door, seemed to be fading, making the climb more challenging. As Nova's foot landed on a solid surface, an ear-splitting noise erupted from the corridor behind them. They both jumped with even more of a jolt than when the school bell chimed. Above the frenzy of the deafening sound, a high-pitched scream resonated through the space.

"What is that?" Nova barely heard herself scream the words. The sound of banging metal echoed up the enclosed stairwell.

Ayden didn't answer. He ripped his hand from hers. She feared she would tumble down the stairs and groped for the handrail. With her free hand, she grasped at the darkness, searching for her friend.

"Ayden! Ayden, where are you?" she screamed.

"Down here."

His figure cut through the murk, backlit by the scarce light from the windows in the hallway. He peered up into the darkness, but Nova knew he couldn't see her.

"What's going on down there?" she yelled.

"You'll have to come see for yourself. Be careful. Can you see me?"

"Yes."

"Keep your eyes on me. You only have a few more stairs."

Chapter 23

Caitlyn did see Nova and Ayden as they slipped past the gymnasium doors. She had no idea what Nova and Ayden were up to, but she knew she had to find out. No one in the gym noticed her leave. She thought she'd been caught as she tiptoed behind them. Not knowing where they were going, she kept moving when the two reached the entrance to the walled-off hall. Fortunately, she was able to duck into an alcove before she was spotted and breathed a sigh of relief as the two disappeared behind the plastic sheet.

She had her phone out, ready to snap a photo of the two sneaking into places they didn't belong. Of course, if she were to call her duet partner out, she'd have to explain what she herself was doing in the closed-off corridor. But that would be easy. She had Ms. Merritt wrapped around her little finger. Maybe if the offense was bad enough, Nova would get disciplined. Everyone knew one disciplinary action could get you booted out of extra-circulars—which would include being taken off the concert choir, leaving Caitlyn to sing a solo after all.

When the principal called her in about the cookie incident with Nova, Caitlyn easily fooled the woman into believing it was nothing but an unintentional mishap. Ms. Merritt went so far as to confide in Caitlyn that she believed the whole food allergy thing was blown out of proportion. She'd never even heard of gluten until Nova's mother threw a fit.

She squeezed through the barrier into the grimy hall that was littered with construction equipment. Fearing even the smallest sound might tip them off, she did her best to move stealthily. When Nova and Ayden disappeared behind a wall in the depths of the corridor, she picked up the pace, rapidly closing the gap.

As she approached the end of the hall, a cold blast of wind confronted her from behind. She turned quickly as a heavy white mist came hurtling down the hall in her direction. She stumbled backward, lost her balance, and fell, landing in a pile of empty boxes. She dropped her phone and it skittered away from her. She wanted to scream but when she opened her mouth, a face emerged from the icy cloud. It rushed toward Caitlyn where she sat, defenseless on the floor.

Hot tears spilled down her face as the figure of a girl materialized from the once-shapeless cloud. The girl herself was misty, like the haze she was formed from. Although the girl wasn't whole, her gauzy shape held a strength that turned Caitlyn's blood cold. As the girl flew toward her, she tried to clamor from her spot on the floor. The boxes slid beneath her feet, leaving her helpless and prone.

The specter bent down and looked into Caitlyn's eyes. She wished she could look away, block the girl's hollow, angry stare, the eyes blue and fiery. The girl opened her mouth and screamed into Caitlyn's face with a force that blew her hair back and lifted tiny bits of dust into a frenzy around her.

The face closed in on Caitlyn, forcing her to inch backward until her back hit a bank of empty lockers. There was nowhere else for her to go. She shrunk into a ball, grabbing her knees, hugging them tightly. Knowing she was trapped, she had no alternative but to find her voice. She took a lengthy inhale and screamed with all her might. The high-pitched keening bounced off the locker-lined walls. She forced her eyes open and watched as the girl's shape morphed again into an angry, roiling cloud that rose above her before once again taking the shape of a girl. The girl floated over her head. Caitlyn sensed this was her chance to run. She crawled across the floor, frantically pushing debris aside, searching for her phone.

But Evelyn wasn't done with Caitlyn yet. The entire space began to vibrate. Sawdust, nails, and papers rose into the air before swirling together in a twisting mass of debris. It reminded Caitlyn of a tornado she'd once seen when visiting her grandparents. Only there was a storm shelter on her Grammy and Pop's ranch. The sounds they heard as she pressed herself tightly against her Grammy and covered her ears were as loud as the uproar she heard in the hall. The lockers that lined the walls slammed open and shut.

Caitlyn wanted nothing more than to be far away from this relentless attack. She managed to find her feet and she ran. She didn't care if she never saw her phone again, didn't care about the trouble she might be in for losing it. All that mattered was that she free herself from this corridor. She ran with all her might, leaping over saws, side-stepping a concrete mixer, and finally bursting through the plastic sheet at the mouth of the hall.

She was running so fast she couldn't slow down in time

to keep from running into a woman standing in the foyer. Her mind barely registered who the person was.

"Sorry," she whispered, breathlessly. She ran straight to the gym where she collapsed against one of the padded walls. Tears spilled down her face.

"Caitlyn, what's wrong?" one of the girls on the squad asked, kneeling next to the shaken girl.

Helpless to stop the tears, powerless to calm her trembling body, and unable to speak, Caitlyn dropped her head to her knees, ignoring everything around her.

Chapter 24

While Nova and Ayden battled the darkness, the meeting with Nurse Brumley came to a close. As the two watched in disbelief the unseen force sparking chaos in the hallway, the nurse made her way out of the office. She didn't bother to check into her own office; the meeting with the principal and vice principal was all she could manage today. Still unsure of her readiness to return to work, she choked back panic and tried to put on a brave face as the discussion of her return played out around her.

It didn't feel real to her. The doctors implored her to accept that her visions were figments of her overburdened mind. Of course, they provided medication to calm her nerves and balance her brain chemistry. She wanted to believe the answer was that simple. A little rest at Health Springs Manor, coupled with meditation and medication, would have her ready to jump back into the life that broke her.

She waved goodbye over her shoulder with a fake smile that threatened to crumble and walked toward the doors of the school. The commotion behind the tarp that covered the hallway stopped her in her tracks. Beads of sweat erupted all over her body. She was mesmerized by the uproar, unable to move. She didn't dare go closer, to peer behind the shroud that blocked her view of the calamity raging behind it. A child's scream permeated the space, rising above the din. Instincts kicked in and she moved to help whoever was caught in the chaos beyond the tarp. As she reached for the opening, bracing herself, a child burst through, almost knocking her to the ground. The girl apologized and before Nurse Brumley could question her, she disappeared down the main corridor.

Quiet descended as the ruckus abruptly ended. She struggled with her will, a voice telling her to run, that nothing good could be lingering in the hall. After all, it was the hallway that led to the bathroom where she held Evelyn Chambers long after the girl took her last breath. But something was calling her. She pushed her way into the hall and was instantly taken back to that awful day.

Chapter 25

"I don't know if this is a good idea, Melanie. What if she gets sick?"

"Shut up! She isn't going to get sick. Well, maybe she'll break out in hives or something. My dad's uncle is allergic to peanuts. His skin just gets all blotchy. It's grody, but it passes."

The two girls were huddled around Melanie's locker. Melanie pulled a bag of peanuts out of her backpack and plucked two nuts out.

"This ought to do it," Melanie said with a grin. She pinched the peanut between her thumb and index finger, eyeing it from every angle like it was a diamond.

Nicole had never seen this look on her friend's face. They'd known each other since before kindergarten. Melanie's expression frightened her; it was menacing, almost evil. She had to look away—the intensity was too much for her. She busied herself picking at a faded sticker on the locker next to Melanie's.

"Are you sure about this, Mel? I mean, what if you get

caught? I know you're mad you didn't get first seat, but there's another audition next semester, and you haven't been playing the violin that long——"

"I don't care about next semester," Melanie hissed. "I've been playing longer than her, and I take private lessons. I deserve first seat, and I plan on being first seat this weekend at the concert. The high school band director will be there, and he needs to see my face in the first chair! This will be just enough to keep her out of first seat so Mr. Garland can see he was wrong to give her the spot. Besides, my plan is foolproof. There's no way we'll get caught. It will be chalked up to an accident or something. Are you with me or not?"

Nicole bore her nails into the sticker, determined to peel it off the locker, giving her time to think about what her best friend intended to do. The plan scared her, but when Melanie was angry, she was scary too. Nicole swallowed hard and nodded her head.

"Good," Melanie retorted. "Malik's birthday is today. His mom brought cupcakes for the class. I overheard Ms. Robinson assuring Evelyn's mom that they didn't have peanuts."

"I know, I know, you've told me a million times."

"Well, it doesn't hurt going over it again. Ms. Robinson always has me help hand things out," Melanie said, rolling her shoulders back and straightening her spine. "So you keep Evelyn distracted while I put the peanut in her cupcake."

Melanie slammed her locker shut, and the two girls walked to their classroom. Nicole was reaching for the door when Melanie grabbed her by the shoulders and whipped her around, so they stood face-to-face.

"Listen, Nicole," she warned, her teeth clenched closely together like a mother scolding her child in public.

"I need you to keep your wits about you and your eyes open. The only way this plan works is if we both do our parts."

"I get it," Nicole said, shrugging her friend's hands off her.

Melanie opened the door and motioned for her friend to go first as the bell rang.

"Happy Birthday, Malik," Melanie said as she made her way to her seat.

Malik pointed at Melanie and winked.

With ten minutes left in the period, Ms. Robinson told the class to put their things away and clear their desks. Giggles and murmurs spread through the room as Ms. Robinson pulled a large bakery box from behind her desk.

"Malik and Melanie, will you two pass the cupcakes out?"

Melanie jumped up from her seat and practically ran to the front of the class. Evelyn Chambers sat in the front row. Melanie gave a steely-eyed glance at her friend and snatched the first cupcake from the box. Nicole tapped on Evelyn's shoulder and the two started talking about Evelyn's sweater. That had been Melanie's idea when Nicole couldn't decide how to strike up a conversation with the shy girl.

Melanie smiled and slipped the peanut under the frosting. Nicole looked on, side-eyeing while making small talk with Evelyn about the sweater. She was amazed at how smooth her friend was. Nicole barely noticed the girl slipping the peanut into the cupcake. If she hadn't known Melanie was doing it, she'd never have noticed the sleight of hand. The cupcakes were topped with cookie crumbles. The peanut would easily pass as a cookie piece; the luck of it all.

When the cupcakes had been handed out, Melanie

returned to her seat, cupcake in hand, and watched as Evelyn took the last bite of hers and neatly folded the paper liner into a tight triangle.

Nicole barely touched her snack. A cold sweat broke out all over her and the sounds of the classroom slipped away, replaced by a ringing in her ears—a siren that warned her this plan was about to go off the rails. If she said anything to Melanie about it, she knew her friend would scoff and call her paranoid. But as the moments ticked by, Nicole was buried under the weight of a bad premonition. She wanted to stand up and scream for Evelyn to go to the nurse, but she didn't have the nerve. Besides, there wasn't any turning back now.

When the bell rang, Nicole heard Evelyn coughing. It sounded like a little cough, the kind that happened when you swallowed funny. She glanced at the girl and saw a lacy red thread erupting on her neck, climbing out of the sweater's collar. Evelyn coughed again and pushed past the kids meandering at the door. She made a beeline for the water faucet and took a long gulp before pushing through the crowds of kids, making her way to the bathroom.

Melanie grabbed Nicole's elbow as they exited the class, pushing her forward.

"Looks like my little plan may be working," she whispered in Nicole's ear. "Let's follow," she said, sliding her hand down to Nicole's hand, gripping it tightly.

Nicole didn't follow Melanie, but rather, was dragged along behind the girl as she pushed her way through groups of students.

"Look, she's going into the grody bathroom," Melanie said before bursting through the bathroom doors. A neon light bulb twitched and buzzed above them, flickering off and on. Evelyn stood at the bank of sinks, splashing cold water on her face.

Melanie broke away from Nicole and went into a stall.

"Those cupcakes were wicked good, right, Nic?" she called from behind the stall door.

"For sure," Nicole replied dreamily. She couldn't take her eyes off Evelyn. The girl was struggling.

"Hey, Evelyn," she started, stepping closer to the sink where Evelyn stood. "Are you OK?"

Evelyn turned to face her, and Nicole couldn't hide the shock that splashed across her face. Evelyn's face was swollen and red. Her eyes bulged, eyes that spoke to Nicole. The only word she managed to eke out was 'help.' Her voice rattled and choked. She tugged at the neck of her sweater, stretching it horribly.

Evelyn grasped the sink basin with one hand and reached for Nicole with the other. Nicole withdrew from the girl, and Evelyn slid to the ground.

"Help," she whispered again, her voice barely perceivable.

"Melanie, you need to get out here!" Nicole yelled, her voice shrill with panic. "Something's wrong!"

"Don't have a cow, Nicole! I'm almost done."

Nicole slid to the floor and picked Evelyn's head up, cradling it in her lap.

"Melanie! Now!"

"Ugh, what's your damage?" Melanie asked, pushing the stall door open. She was tucking her Oxford into her jeans but stopped in mid-tuck. She froze and stood staring.

"Go get the nurse, or someone, anyone!" Nicole yelled at her.

Nicole's voice seemed to break the spell that fell over Melanie. Melanie crumbled to the floor next to Nicole and Evelyn. Evelyn was gasping. Her expression was twisted in pain and panic, her eyes pleading, her skin an ugly purple, her lips colorless.

Melanie grabbed Evelyn's arms and shook her. Evelyn's head lolled and her limbs flailed limply like a rag doll.

"Snap out of it, Evelyn!" she said. "We get it! You got us! This isn't funny! You can stop now. We'll never bother you again. You can have the stupid first seat."

Tears flooded Melanie's eyes before spilling down her face.

"What do we do, Melanie?"

"I don't know! Let me think."

Melanie gently released Evelyn's upper body before getting up and turning the faucet on in the sink closest to where they huddled. She cupped as much as her hands could hold and did her best to splash the cooling liquid over Evelyn's face. It had no effect. The girl's muscles were stiff; she shook with violent tremors. All Nicole could do was to hold onto her. She shushed her continually even though the girl wasn't making any noise, none that she had control of anyway.

"Go get someone! Now!" Nicole screamed.

Melanie bent down again, her face mere inches from Nicole's.

"I can't go get someone! Do you know what happens to us if anyone finds out we did this?" she hissed.

Nicole dropped her head, tears overtaking her. She despised the words us and we. She didn't want to be a part of this nightmare and had no reply for her friend. Sobs overcame her.

While Nicole cried and hushed the now-silent Evelyn, Melanie stood up. She checked herself in the mirror, angrily wiping the tears from her face before tucking her shirt in and smoothing her hair. She didn't say another word. She simply walked out of the bathroom, leaving Nicole alone with the dying girl.

For some time, Nicole believed Melanie had gone for help. She expected adults to burst through the door and free her of the literal death grip she had on Evelyn Chambers. When she heard the bell ring for the next period, and again for the one after that, she gave up hope. The world outside the dreary bathroom ceased to exist. The buzzing fluorescent light flickering on and off and a dripping faucet were the only things that kept her grounded. The frenzied rush outside the door marking students passing to their next class became nothing more than white noise, a murmur that seeped through the bathroom walls like ghosts she left behind in another life. The life that forever changed when she ducked inside this bathroom.

Her mind was consumed by one fervent wish—that she could go back in time and stop all of this from happening. Never had she wanted anything more. Still, she could not force herself up off the floor, could not make herself abandon the dead girl. She didn't want to admit that she was dead, but some nagging little voice in the farthest reaches of her mind told her Evelyn was gone. She clung to the belief that if she only kept a hold on the poor girl, she could keep her there, tethered to life, tethered to hope.

As the day passed, Evelyn Chambers grew cold. When the final bell rang, hope drained from Nicole. She gently lifted Evelyn's head from her lap, placed it gently on the ground, and stood. Pins and needles burst like fireworks in her legs and feet. She shook them, urging them to wake up, begging the numbness to dissipate. She didn't dare look in the mirror, certain she'd find a monster staring back at her. A monster who took the life of an innocent girl, a girl no older than herself.

The buzzing flash of the overhead tube light almost brought life to Evelyn. Bright light dimming suddenly worked the shadows that fell across her cold, blue face. It was too frightening for Nicole to bear anymore.

"I'm so sorry," she whispered to the dead girl. Then she ran from the room.

Chapter 26

Nicole Brumley pounded her fists against her head as if she could chase the horrible memory away with her blows. She turned to leave the hallway when she heard a voice, a faint calling. She turned back and stared down the long passage. Outside, the sun dropped away from the sky and the hall fell even darker. She held her breath, listening for the voice again. Right when she convinced herself her mind was playing more cruel tricks on her, she heard it again.

"Help me," a voice whispered from the far end of the hall. Instinct pushed her forward. She was a nurse. If a child was in trouble, she would be the one to help. Slowly she walked down the hall, winding her way through the maze of construction materials. Each time she paused, the voice cried out to her.

She reached the stairwell and looked up in time to see someone slip behind the door at the top. Taking a deep breath and pushing out the voice in her head that screamed at her to turn back, she lifted a foot and ascended the dark staircase.

Ms. Merritt returned to her office, pleased the meeting went well. Her concern that Nicole still wasn't ready to return seemed to be unfounded. Dropping into her chair, she moved her computer's mouse to wake the monitor up. She was immediately drawn into the screen, her eyes wide as she scanned the different views of the halls, classrooms, and exterior areas of the school. The new security system and cameras fascinated her. She was excited to know she could be in many places at once, without ever leaving her office. Her attention went to the monitor that showed the hallway being renovated. She stared in disbelief as the lockers slammed open and shut. One lone child ran through the hall. It was a girl, but she struggled to place her. The girl was wearing a cheer uniform, making her all the more anonymous.

She did recognize the person who entered the hallway after the girl made her way free of the plastic sheeting. It was Nicole.

"What are you doing in there, Nicole?" she asked an empty room.

She quickly locked her screen and skirted around her desk. Nicole had no business being in the work zone. Maybe she was wrong about the nurse being better. Whatever the case was, she wasn't going to let Nicole linger there any longer.

As she exited her office, Mrs. Yates, the secretary, was gathering her jacket and purse.

"Have a good night, Ms. Merritt," the woman said as the principal rushed past her and slammed into the door. Stepping back just in time not to be hit in the face, the lunch lady stood there.

"Excuse you," Mel said.
Ms. Merritt didn't reply.

Chapter 27

Nova and Ayden stood and watched the activity in the hallway quiet in an instant as if a switch were flipped after Caitlyn bolted through the tarp.

"Um, that was wild," Ayden said. "Did we just see that, or are we in some nightmare rotation?"

"Yeah," Nova replied, "Evelyn Chambers is not a big fan of Caitlyn Rogers."

"Not going to ask how you know that. I'll take your word. But listen, this is getting pretty creepy. What if someone heard all of that? I think we should call this thing off. Too much weirdness. I'm not down with this vibe."

Nova found a determination she didn't know existed in her.

"No, I'm not leaving now! We've made it this far. I'm not giving up. You don't have to come with me, but I'm getting into that attic today. Something, I don't know what or how or why, but something is telling me this is the only way for me to say goodbye to Evelyn Chambers. I can't live like this any longer. She visits me in my nightmares. She sits on the bus with me. It's too much! I want my life back."

"Alright, alright, I'm with you. Let's find out what is up there. But if—" Ayden didn't finish his sentence. A voice interrupted him. It was Evelyn Chambers calling for help. "Hold up, did you hear that?"

"It's Evelyn. We can't back out now. Let's do this," she whispered. She reached her hand out to her friend. He took it, and she found his palms to be as clammy as hers. She knew he was scared, but she needed his strength to go forward.

Nova held tight to Ayden's hand as they climbed the stairs. When they reached the top, they found a small landing. It was too small for them to stand together. Nova slid the necklace over her head and found the key. With shaky hands, she pushed it into the lock. The old lock creaked as Nova turned the key. She heard a click and the door flew open. There was light in the room, coming from a bright white aura surrounding Evelyn Chambers.

The glow was welcoming, like she was greeting them. From behind her, Nova heard Ayden gasp. He tugged on her hand as if he wanted to encourage her to head back down the stairs. She pulled her fingers from his grip and walked slowly toward the girl in the center of the cramped attic.

The two girls stood facing each other in the musty space. Nova solid and centered; Evelyn a misty figure that defied gravity and flickered in and out of sight like a candle flame being hushed by a breeze. They stood so close that Nova could reach out and touch the hazy girl, but she hoped it wouldn't come to that. Fear was creeping in on her; its icy hand slithered up her spine. This was almost too much to believe. There had never been a plan past the point where they made it into the attic. Nova wasn't sure what to do next.

Still, the mysterious specter's voice was loud enough;

the nearly invisible presence strong enough that she led Nova to this neglected space for the sole purpose of telling the story about her tragic end. Beyond the shadowy figure, Nova didn't notice the letters and numbers scratched into the wooden wall until Evelyn Chambers made her way to hover next to it. The girl didn't walk; she didn't float either. Her form jumped from space to space. She disappeared, then reappeared at a different spot in the room.

Nova moved slowly like she was walking underwater. When she reached the wall, a sense of knowing settled in her bones. The sparse information scrawled in the wood might not make sense to some. Nova immediately grasped the meaning and knew those few carved lines would change the lives of many people. She also knew the scrawled writing would set free the spirit that haunted her for weeks. All Evelyn Chambers ever wanted was for someone to know who was responsible for her untimely death.

Ayden hadn't moved beyond the threshold of the door. He stood, mouth dropped open, shaking his head. A noise behind them broke his trance-like gaze.

"Nova," he whispered. "Someone is coming!"

"Close the door," she whispered back to him, never taking her eyes off the girl.

The hinges let out a keening moan before clicking back into place. Nova believed the noise was made by Ayden closing the door until she heard a sharp, gasping inhale behind her.

"You found her," the voice said.

Nova turned to see Nurse Brumley standing in the doorway. Ayden stood where Nova left him. He shrugged his shoulders. Nurse Brumley stepped forward on shaky legs. She clasped her hand over her mouth and let out a choked sob. Behind her the door slammed, the sound resonating through the attic. The jarring strike jolted Nurse Brumley and she backed away, her hand grasping behind her searching for the doorknob. She found the knob and pulled, but the door wouldn't budge.

"Please don't hurt me, Evelyn!" she pleaded. "I'm so sorry. I'm sorry I didn't help you. I've lived with this regret for so long." As she spoke, Nurse Brumley moved away from the door and slowly made her way to the wall.

She inched closer to Nova and took the girl's hand. Tears streamed down her face. Nova held Nurse Brumley's hand, but the woman shrunk to the floor. She read the words on the wall silently, her lips moving, her voice unheard.

"That's the day, the day it all happened," Nurse Brumley whispered as her fingers traced the last line of writing. She looked up at Nova. "It wasn't supposed to end that way. It was just a prank. A stupid, mean prank."

Ayden approached Nurse Brumley.

"Let me help you up, Mrs. Brumley," he said, taking the woman's hand. She didn't rise but squeezed his hand tightly and looked up at him.

"Only a prank," she whispered.

Suddenly, the door to the attic crashed open and a fierce wind whipped through the small space. Evelyn Chambers was gone from the spot she was hovering over and reappeared high above them all. She flew down from the rafters, but she was no longer the shape of a timid, young girl. Her form was enlarged and distorted. Red eyes burned from her face, which was twisted with rage. A silent scream blasted the face of the person standing in the doorway. It was Ms. Merritt. The woman's hair lifted from her shoulders and was tossed about in the angry gale sparked by Evelyn.

Nurse Brumley rose from the floor, aided by Nova and Ayden.

"Look at the wall," she said. Nurse Brumley's voice so low and faint, barely a whisper, unheard by Nova and Ayden. But not by Evelyn Chambers, it seemed. Her distorted and terrifying figure shrank and disappeared as if sucked into a vacuum. When she reappeared, she was face-to-face with the woman in the doorway.

Ayden broke the silence. "Ms. Merritt, I can explain." Nova gave him a sharp glance and mouthed the words, 'Not now.' Ayden fell quiet.

"Come see. Look what she wrote on the wall."

"What is going on in here?" Ms. Merritt snapped. "Nicole, why are you up here? What are you two doing here? What exactly is going on?"

"She led us here. It wasn't all in my head. All this time, she's been trying to get my attention. There is something she needs to show us. Come, see." Nurse Brumley walked to Ms. Merritt and took her by the hand.

"Nicole, what is this nonsense?" Ms. Merritt hissed, yanking her hand free.

"Look, look here." Nurse Brumley moved toward the wall, turning back and gesturing with her arm for Ms. Merritt to follow.

"I'll have none of this. I don't know what you are all up to, but this behavior will be punished. Suspension is a definite, and expulsion might not be—"

Before she could finish, Evelyn Chambers appeared again. This time she stood behind Ms. Merritt and the woman lurched forward, pushed from behind. When she found her balance, Ms. Merritt turned to look behind her. Evelyn Chambers materialized to a more solid shape than Nova had ever seen. It was as if she were alive and as solid and real as any of the others who were drawn to this room.

"Evelyn," she whispered. "How?"

Ms. Merritt moved to the wall without any further prodding by Nurse Brumley or Evelyn Chambers. Her eyes fell on the wall. She gasped and her knees buckled, all the strength in her was overtaken by gravity. Ayden stepped in to catch her before she fell to the ground.

She looked into the boys' eyes, color drained from her face, and her lips trembled when she said.

"Who did this?" she asked. "I don't understand."

"Evelyn Constance Chambers, October fourteenth, nineteen-seventy," Nova read from the wall.

"That was her birthday," said Nurse Brumley. "I've visited her grave often."

"Read the next line, Nova," Ayden said. His eyes hadn't left Ms. Merritt's face.

"I died on November first, nineteen-eighty-three," Nova continued.

"Stop! Stop this nonsense right now!" Ms. Merritt spoke in her most authoritative voice, but it fell flat. It didn't carry the weight that it did when she told people to stop running in the hall.

"She can't stop," Nurse Brumley said.

"Melinda Ann Merritt. It was not an accident."

Ms. Merritt rushed to Nova and grabbed the girl by the shoulders.

"Who did this?" she yelled in Nova's face, shaking her. "Why would you write something so, so … You vindictive child!

Nurse Brumley stepped between Nova and Ms. Merritt, removing the woman's grip from Nova's shoulders as she did.

"It wasn't Nova, Melinda," Nurse Brumley said. "It's time the world knew."

"Stop it, Nicole!" the woman screamed. "There is nothing for anyone to know!"

"Mel, come on. We both know what you did. It's time to take responsibility."

"What I did? Don't you mean what—"

The room vibrated, and a thick coat of dust that had settled and grown over the years bounced from every surface. The white glow around Evelyn Chambers turned a fiery red. She swooped down from the rafters again in a blur before she stopped, standing eye-to-eye with Ms. Merritt.

"This is ludicrous," Ms. Merritt screamed, her voice barely rising above the loud energy of the space. She turned and ran toward the door. It slammed in her face, stopping her momentum. The collision threw her back, and she landed at Nurse Brumley's feet.

The nurse sank to the floor and took Ms. Merritt's hands.

"Melinda, we've kept this secret buried too long. We won't be able to put it behind us until we confess. It's time. You need to own what you did."

"What we did, you mean," her words rushed out in an angry shriek. "I wasn't alone in this, Nicole! You could have stopped me."

"Maybe," Nurse Brumley replied.

"You could have stopped me, and you didn't get any help for her. You sat there and watched her die!"

Nova and Ayden stood huddled together. Nova couldn't believe the scene unfolding in front of them. The principal, Ms. Merritt, was the one who devised a plan to hurt poor Evelyn Chambers. She was also the one who walked away from the tragedy she created and went about her life as if nothing ever happened.

Nurse Brumley reached for Ms. Merritt and drew her

near. The principal gave in to the embrace, and the two women held each other. Their sobs were the only noise in the small space until another sound rose above their weeping. A scratching, as if a mouse was constructing an escape through the wall.

Nova and Ayden turned to the sound. In front of their eyes, the words appeared, scratched into the wood by an unseen hand.

The words *thank you* were already etched; the letters stood out clearly as the new carving broke the flesh of the ancient wooden plank on which they were inscribed. Slowly more letters appeared. Tears streamed down Nova's face as the letters formed T-H-A-N-K-Y-O-U-N-O-V-A.

As the final A took shape before their eyes, the buzzing energy that filled the room dissipated. Darkness shrouded the space and Nova sensed, for the first time since she arrived at Westland Park, a calmness, a peace. She was no longer tethered to the long-dead girl. Evelyn Chambers was finally heard, and the ghost girl had moved on.

____

Chapter 28

____

Backstage buzzed with excitement. A nervous energy coursed through the students as they prepared to walk on stage and perform their concert for an audience. Hushed murmurs vibrated below the sharp voices of Mrs. Hastings and the stagehands.

Nova and Caitlyn sat next to each other as they applied stage makeup. Their mirrored faces appeared harsh under the intense glow of the rounded light bulbs that ringed them.

"Easy on the blush, Nova," Caitlyn said. "You want to look natural, not like a clown."

Nova set the makeup brush on the vanity, looked at Caitlyn's mirrored image, and stuck her tongue out.

"What do you have against clowns?"

"I don't have anything against clowns. But the theme is a day in the park, not a day at the circus. Just saying." Now Caitlyn stuck her tongue out at Nova's mirror face, and they both erupted in laughter.

"Stop making me laugh," Caitlyn pleaded. "My mascara is going to smudge!"

The two worked hard on their duet and knew they both had the same goal in mind, a flawless performance. As they worked toward this shared desire, they put aside their differences and even grew to like each other.

The two girls saw Ayden approach and burst into laughter again. They had never seen him in his beekeeper costume, and it was quite a sight. A floppy white hat draped in mesh sat atop his head, making him taller than he already was. He carried a bee smoker, and as he approached Nova and Caitlyn, he smashed the bellow dramatically. The girls cringed, trying to avoid the "smoke" that spewed from the can. It was only baby powder. The fine dust rained down on the girls as they batted it away and choked on talcum-induced laughter.

"Cut it out, Ayden!" Caitlyn cried. "You're going to mess up my hair!"

"You're also going to run out of powder before your big moment. Did you ever get your line memorized?" Nova asked.

"Lines, I think is what you meant. I have multiple lines. Some might say I carry this show."

The girls rolled their eyes and turned back to the mirror.

"How about you *buzz* off and practice those lines so we can finish our makeup?" Caitlyn joked.

"I see what you did there, Cait," Ayden replied. "Good one."

The lights backstage flashed twice and dimmed. Mrs. Hastings popped her head into the makeshift staging room.

"Places, everyone," she whispered. "Break a leg!"

A flurry of activity erupted as kids took their spots. As they walked on the stage, Mrs. Simmons spoke into a microphone.

"Welcome, welcome everyone, to our Spring Fling

concert! I'd like to take a moment to thank you all for coming. These kids have been busy as bees preparing for this show."

From the apron, a drum started up as the spotlight focused on Ayden. He struggled to free himself of the curtains and find his mark. Once onstage, he sprayed the front row seats with his baby powder bee smoke. The drumroll ended with a rim shot. Mrs. Simmons waited for the laughter to die down, suppressing her laughter as she watched her son fight his way back through the curtains before she continued.

"Let's give a big round of applause to our fabulous music teacher, Mrs. Hastings! Come on out here, Mrs. Hastings, and take a bow!"

Mrs. Hastings jogged onto the stage, clipboard in hand, stopwatch swinging madly around her neck, looking very flustered as she curtsied before running off stage.

"I know the past few weeks have been a bit of a challenge for our Panthers. Thank you all for welcoming me as your new principal. I am honored and excited to serve this wonderful school. After the show, please take a few minutes to walk around the school and check out the newly renovated entry hall and library. And stop by the cafeteria for some gluten and allergen-free refreshments! Now, without further ado, please welcome to the stage the Panthers' Concert Choir as they bring you the songs and dances of spring!"

The students took their spots on the risers as Mrs. Hastings played a tune on the piano. The audience murmured as they spotted their child or grandchild and waved, while the flash of dozens of cameras created a strobe light effect through the darkened auditorium.

Mrs. Hastings rose from the piano and tapped out a beat, her arms in the air as she conducted the opening number. Nova sang along, a smile on her face as she scanned the crowd looking for her mom. When she located her mom in the third row, she noticed who was sitting next to her. It was Nan. Nova's smile widened as the last beat of the song rang out.

The audience applauded, and Nova and Caitlyn stepped down from the risers and clasped hands before walking to the microphone. When the applause died down, the girls inhaled, and on the exhale, their voices merged in perfect harmony. By the end of the song, the crowd was on their feet. Nova and Caitlyn bowed graciously and stepped back to their spots on the risers.

After the concert, Nova wound her way through the throngs of parents, grandparents, uncles and aunts, and older and younger siblings. She saw her mom, bouncing up and down and waving a hand, and she ran to her and threw her arms around her.

"I brought a special guest," her mom said, as she released Nova from the hug.

"Nan! I'm so happy you came!" Nova said, throwing her arms gently around the fragile woman.

Nan held a bouquet of spring flowers wrapped neatly and tied with a purple string.

"Wouldn't have missed it for anything, Nova," she said, handing over the flowers.

"Thank you, Nan! They're beautiful!" Nova put her face in the bundle and breathed deeply.

"Listen, I'm parched," Nan said. "Let's make our way to the cafeteria. I hear they're handing out gluten-free cookies, I know those are your favorite."

The threesome made their way to the cafeteria. Conversations swirled around them. Nova's ears homed in on as many snippets as she could decipher. She and Ayden had their names left out of the official story. Ms. Merritt resigned from her position at the school.

"I hear the police are conducting an investigation," a faceless woman's voice whispered behind Nova.

"The whole thing is an utter disgrace," opined a man as he poured lemonade into a paper cup.

"It's just so hard to believe! She was such a nice woman and a great leader," Nova overheard as she made her way to the table she and Ayden claimed as their own on Nova's first day.

"It'll be tough to get charges that stick. It happened so long ago," an older man said.

"They should just let sleeping dogs lie," a woman said as Nova squeezed past her, trying not to spill the cups of lemonade she balanced in both hands. Ayden followed behind her, his hands full of cookies.

"Mrs. Eckley, I didn't know you were bringing your sister," Ayden said as he slid into a seat at the table.

Nova rolled her eyes and let out a groan while Nan batted her eyelashes. It was good to see her grandma so clear-headed.

Ayden took a bite of a cookie, and his eyes widened.

"You gotta try these cookies," he said. "You'd never guess they're missing all that gluten."

Acknowledgments

The list of people I owe sincere gratitude to gets longer with each book. First, to my family, without your support and enthusiasm, none of my stories would be told. Thank you for putting up with me as I ask the same question hundreds of times and repeat the same narratives again and again. You all are my only reason.

As usual, tremendous gratitude to my editing team. Michele and Andrea, I hold you and the team members of Two Birds Author Service in high regard. You have the amazing ability to make my stories the best they can be and for that, I thank you.

I reached out to the celiac community and had the great fortune to build an amazing beta team for this book. Hailey Hipwood, Lizzy McCall and Faith Costa read the rough draft of the book and provided in-depth opinions and insightful suggestions. I was blown away by these three young ladies! Remember their names ... they will go far! Hailey, Lizzy and Faith, I cannot thank you enough!

Lastly, many thanks to my great friends in the SHS graduating class of 1986. Mary, Ann, Maggie, Elisabeth, Chrissi, Judy, Ginger, Lana and Melanie ... your support and encouragement has done wonders for my confidence. You will never know how grateful I am for having such a great cheering section!

As always, hugs and thanks to Jordan, Zoe and Dar!

Shout out to @pizza_wednesday

Also By Lisa Courtaway

Red Water - Shadows of Camelot Crossing, A Haunting in Stillwater, Book 1

Deep Water - Shadows of Camelot Crossing, A Haunting in Stillwater, Book 2

About the Author

Lisa Courtaway lives in Stillwater, Oklahoma and is married with four children. An entourage of six dogs follows her everywhere. She has worn many career-hats, from advertising to insurance to education. Currently she is writing the third book in the Shadows of Camelot Crossing series and dreaming up a story for her second Haunted Hallways Mystery series.

She loves a good ghost story, and has lived in several homes that spoke to her in mysterious ways. True crime stories, watching a binge-worthy series, reading, and lovingly meddling in the lives of her children are her favorites.

Since she was young, people have often told her she should write a book ... so she did ... and then did it again ... and again ... and she plans to keep doing so.

You can find out more about Lisa, including her social media links and content, at her website:

www.lisacourtaway.com